CW01573539

# NEVER ALONE

## A Journey into Mediumship

Amy Dium

Casdec Ltd

Copyright 2003 by Amy Dium

First published in Great Britain by Casdec Ltd Oct.2003

The right of Amy Dium to be identified as the author of the work has been asserted by her in accordance with the Copyright, Designs and Patents act 1988.

All rights reserved. No part of this publication may be reproduced, stored in a retrieval system, or transmitted, in any form or by any means without the prior written permission of the publisher, nor otherwise be circulated in any form of binding or cover other than that in which it is published and without similar conditions being imposed on the subsequent purchaser.

A CIP catalogue record for this title is available from the
British Library

ISBN 1 900 456141

Printed and bound in Great Britain by
Casdec Ltd, 21/22 Harraton Terrace, Birtley, Co. Durham DH3 2QG

Published by:
Casdec Ltd
21/22 Harraton Terrace
Birtley
Co. Durham
DH3 2QG

up with an explanation why the roses should have changed colour while Amy had been to church, but they all failed.

*"Probably Geoff's way of saying that he's glad you've gone back to church,"* suggested Teresa.

The following day Maria came for a visit. She suggested that Amy should take a photograph of the flowers to prove that they had indeed changed colour. Then the comedy of errors commenced.

First Amy had no film in the camera, so they had to wait until they returned from shopping. Maria wanted to buy a tree to plant in Geoff's memory, so they went to the garden centre as well as the shopping centre. They were hungry when they returned home, so it was some time before Amy got round to taking photographs.

First the camera would not work at all then it fell off the arm of Geoff's chair while Amy was arranging the layout of the intended photograph, with Geoff's picture beside the vase of roses.

*"I don't want to worry you, mam,"* laughed Maria, "*but the roses are turning pink again."*

This made Amy more flustered and she perched on the arm of a chair to take the photograph.

*"I've never seen such an easy task made so difficult,"* laughed Maria. *"It's as if somebody did not want you to take the picture."*

The following week Amy took her first service since Geoff had died. It was in the church where his funeral service had been held and another medium acted as chairperson in case Amy was not up to doing the service alone. This gesture was much appreciated, but Amy found an inner strength that night which she felt came from Geoff. As she stepped down from the platform of the church, she felt the warm glow in her chest and knew that Mr. Latimer approved also.

It was some weeks before Amy developed the film. She had no confidence that the photographs would adequately show the change of colour, but they did. They were not a deep violet, as they had been on the day after she had been to church, but they were a definite lilac. One thing was certain. They were not pink.

Since that time Amy has bought roses regularly from the same supermarket and they have all remained pink. So why did that particular spray suddenly change colour? There may be a simple reason, but Amy has failed to find one. However, as a Spiritualist, she feels that it was Geoff's way of showing her that she is never alone. Bearing in mind the comfort she received from this and other phenomena she has experienced since she became a Spiritualist, who would want to argue?

TO

MY FRIENDS

IN

DEED

And to Stan,
who ignited the spark.

# Introduction

What does a middle aged woman do when she suddenly begins to experience psychic phenomena? When an unseen presence visits her each night? Was she dreaming? She did not think so. The presence seemed very real to her and she felt that there was little chance that she had imagined it, as her dog was aware of it, too. Despite her initial fear, Amy's reaction was to attempt to discover and understand what was happening to her. She was a woman who was used to being in control: she would not be satisfied until she was in possession of all the evidence and able to deal with and control the phenomena she was experiencing.

She was to embark on journey of discovery which would change her life forever. This was a life that she had never imagined for herself and completely alien to anything she had known. It would alter her outlook and give her a new reason for living. It was not an easy journey: many would have abandoned it because at times it seemed that she was making no progress. There appeared to be no purpose, but Amy felt that it was a journey that she had to make.

Her story could be that of any medium, which is why there are no place names, other than the Arthur Findlay College, in the book. Many of the names of the characters have also been changed. What happened to Amy has happened and will happen to mediums all over the world, although there will be variations according to their lifestyle and opportunities. They may all have reacted differently and they may not have taken the same route as Amy, but would have done what they themselves needed to do in order to progress along their individual pathway.

There will also be many others who have had similar psychic experiences and kept them secret, or not investigated to find out their cause or meaning. Whatever their reasons, they may identify with Amy's feelings as she explored the phenomena, taking wrong turns in her ignorance, then finding herself guided towards enlightenment and discovery.

Amy did not always understand what was happening to her and often did things which later proved to be unwise. She is the first to admit that this was because of her own ignorance. Information in this book could have been corrected, or Amy's actions altered to make her appear perfect or knowledgeable, but that was not how it happened. She reacted to situations using the information she had available to her at the time. I feel that her conclusions and reactions illustrate the difficulty that mediums have as they struggle to come to terms with and handle their gift. She wrote her narrative at the time, or soon after, the events happened, so they were fresh in her mind. Because of this, I have endeavoured to reproduce her story as closely as possible.

Amy is an intelligent woman who is not easily led. She always tries to be objective and to examine all evidence available to her before she accepts anything. Look at this evidence yourself, and see what you would have done in Amy's position.

# Prologue

She reached out in a frantic attempt to prevent herself from toppling over the edge: her fingers desperately clawed the air as she plunged in a downward spiral into a seemingly bottomless abyss. Arms flailing, she tried to slow her fall, but there were no sides to touch, nothing but a swirling mass, dragging her into oblivion. She braced herself for the shock of landing then woke with a start. Her initial feeling of relief was short lived as the grim reality of what she had done flooded her consciousness. Horror and disgust swept over her as she realised she was lying in a pool of urine and cold sweat.

"*Please, let me be dreaming,*" she prayed silently.

The rhythmical sound of her younger brothers' breathing, as they slept in the double bed a few feet away, confirmed she was awake. This was no dream, and she would have to face the consequences of what she had done.

She was unable to do anything about her discomfort, for there were no clean sheets. Even if there had been more bedding, she would not have been able to get it without waking her mother, which would hasten her punishment. She would be thirteen in a couple of months and too old to be wetting the bed. Her mother was certain to give her a good hiding in the morning. Suddenly, the bed did not seem such a bad place to be. It was better to stay where she was, at least until the morning.

The eldest of four children, she lived with her mother, sister and two brothers in two damp, vermin infested rooms in a terraced street near a large river in a British industrial city. The river was dirty, polluted by industrial waste from the factories lining its banks and it was in one of these that the girl's mother worked.

Ten days after her youngest brother was born, the girl's father deserted his family. She was only five at the time, too young to understand why he had gone, yet old enough to miss him. Her siblings remembered little of their father: she was the only one with any real memories of him: the only one who ever asked when he was coming back.

As soon as she was able to write, she sent him letters, asking him to come home. He never replied, but that did not deter her. She continued to write and still waited hopeful for his reply. In her child's mind there was always a possibility of a happy ending and the one sided correspondence continued for many years. She was too young to understand the complexities of adult relationships: that her father may have thought that her mother had dictated the letters.

No matter how hard she tried, she could not get back to sleep. Dreading the approach of morning, she lay awake, thoughts crowding her mind. Her head felt like a tightly wound clock and eventually she found it painful to think at all.

She had been feeling tired and listless for some weeks and had no appetite. Her mother, harassed by the double workload of holding down a job and raising her family without a husband, had eventually found the time to take her to the doctor. As the family doctor was on holiday, his locum examined the girl. He had not seen her before, and had no knowledge of the family's living conditions. Nothing in his medical training or middle class background prepared him for the sight of the girl as she entered his surgery.

"*What's the matter with her?*" he asked, regarding the girl with concern. *"Has she got a cough?"*

The mother pushed the girl forward. *"Answer the doctor."* she commanded. Then, as the girl shook her head, *"No, she never coughs. She just complains of being tired, and she won't eat anything."*

*"What about phlegm?"* he asked. *"Has she brought any up? Has she been spitting?"*

*"No, I've never seen her spit at all."*

*"She's very thin."*

*"She's always been like that. She takes after her father."* Somehow, the mother managed to make these words sound like an insult.

*"Well, then. Let's see if we can find out what's wrong with her."* He took the girl's hand and drew her closer. *"Open wide. Ah! There's the problem. No wonder she has no appetite. Her tonsils are red and very swollen."*

He leafed through the girl's notes on his desk, which showed that she regularly suffered from tonsillitis and was currently awaiting surgery.

*"I'll give you a prescription for penicillin lozenges. They should clear it up. Give her soft foods, such as soup, until the soreness has gone. She should be as right as rain in a week or so; a fortnight at the most. I'll give you a note for school for two weeks."*

*"Thank you, doctor."* The mother took the prescription and bundled her daughter out of the surgery, anxious to take up as little of the busy doctor's precious time as possible, and relieved that her child's illness was not serious.

That had been almost four weeks ago. Instead of improving, the girl gradually deteriorated, but the change was so slight that it was not immediately apparent to those who saw her on a daily basis. By this time her mother's patience was beginning to wear thin. Hadn't she enough to do without having to cope with a so-called sick child moping around the house all day? She'd never been able to talk to her eldest daughter, who was the image of the man who had left her to raise four children on her own. There had always been a lack of understanding, an invisible barrier between them. Exasperated, she asked her current man friend to have a word with the girl.

At first he was sympathetic and his voice was gentle as he spoke. Still, the girl felt awkward and embarrassed to speak to him. He was not her father: he was not even a relation. She resented him becoming involved in family business that should not concern him.

*"What's wrong with you?"* he asked. *"Don't you want to go to school? Is the work too hard for you?"*

She shook her head and remained silent, staring at him sullenly. She could not understand how she could feel so bad without anyone being able to recognise that she was ill. Why did they not believe her? Why did they always have to look for an ulterior motive behind her actions? Did they not realise that she loved going to school? It was a place that offered her a temporary escape, a refuge from her dreary life at home. There she could dream; pretend; hope that one day she would be able to change her life by working hard and passing her exams. Every morning she had forced herself to make the climb up the steep bank to catch the bus to school, until eventually her arms and legs had become like leaden weights: too great a burden for her skinny frame.

How could this man, or her mother, know what an effort it had been for her? They both left early for work in the morning before she got up, leaving her to see to her brothers before setting off to school herself. Sometimes her brothers' reluctance to go to school made her late, for which she received demerit marks against her house, which made her unpopular with the girls in her class who were in the same house. How could they understand her problems? They all had two parents, and a mother at home to see that they were in time for school.

She had passed the scholarship (later known as the eleven plus) and won a place at one of the best grammar schools in the area. The other girls looked down on her because of her shabby, ill fitting, second hand uniform, but that did not deter her from working hard to become one of the brightest girls in the class. She was proud when she finished second top of the class after the first year exams and looked forward eagerly to being promoted to the 'A' class. Then the teacher announced the names of the three girls who would be promoted and she was not included.

Innocently, she asked why, and the teacher told her that one girl in the class had been absent through illness for some of the school year, and would probably have finished in a higher position if her work had not been interrupted. The girl was puzzled, for she had finished second: surely the girl who had finished third should have been the one to lose her place. Her classmates were not as polite as she was, and soon let her know that she had been passed over because of her poor background and shabby appearance. Each of them, regardless of academic achievements, was considered to have more chance of making something of their education than she had.

She was an incurable optimist, and thought that if she could be top of the class in the next exams they would have to promote her. With this in mind she had begun her second year determined to succeed. She enjoyed learning. The work presented a challenge to which her quick mind responded, and her marks were excellent.

*"If there's nothing wrong at school, why are you staying off?"* he went on, his voice becoming harsh as he lost patience with her. He believed that any form of higher education was wasted on girls, especially one who stayed away from school. *"The doctor said you would be better in a fortnight. That was nearly a month ago. You'll have the school board man around after you, and your mother will get into trouble if you stay off school for nothing. Not only that, you're wasting a good education. There's many who would jump at the chance you have. You're keeping somebody out of a place at that school who would appreciate it."*

*"I don't feel well"* pleaded the girl. *"I'm tired all the time."*

Her voice grated in his ears like a whine from a dog. He was sick of her lame excuses. He had no time for malingerers, and did not know why he was bothering with her. After all, she was not even his child.

*"I'm tired,"* he yelled, *"Your mother's tired. We still have to go to work. There's nothing wrong with you that a bit of fresh air won't cure. Instead of lying about the house all day, why don't you*

*go out for a change? Get the stink blown off you."*

Red faced with annoyance, he went into the other room to talk to her mother. They did not attempt to lower their voices, so the girl heard every word as they discussed her.

*"I don't think there's anything wrong with her. I think she's just making it all up,"* he said. *"It's more than likely that she can't keep up with the others at school. They're all clever there, and she's not a big fish in a little puddle any more. She's not used to having to work hard to keep up with the rest, and she's looking for an excuse to stay off. She tells that many lies that you don't know when to believe her. Didn't she come home with a cock and bull story about being put up to the 'A' class? Then why is she still in the 'B' class? I'm telling you, she lives in a dream world, that girl. It's about time she began to grow up and act her age."*

*"But she's lost so much weight."* The mother protested.

*"She will lose weight if she refuses to eat."* He was losing patience with the mother now, believing that she was as much to blame as the girl. *"You're too soft with her, and she takes advantage of you. If you ask me, I think she's a hypochondriac."*

The girl understood the meaning of the word, and felt helpless. What did she have to do to make them believe her? Couldn't they see she was telling the truth? They misinterpreted her lethargy for laziness, something that was not tolerated by the working classes. Saddened, she resolved to try to go to school in the morning. If only she had some energy. Perhaps if she went to bed early she would feel better in the morning.

That had been last night. Now the smell of the wet bed surrounded her. She wished she could stop peeing the bed. She never knew she was doing it until she woke up wet. The doctor had diagnosed a weak bladder and said that she would grow out of it. If only she could. Then, perhaps, she would be able to sleep at her grandmother's house, as her sister did.

As dawn was breaking, she began to fret, dreading the moment when her mother would discover the wet bed. Then she noticed that the door appeared to open. She had not heard her mother get up, but braced herself for what was to come. She wanted to hide, but found she could not move. Like a mesmerised rabbit, she stared at the door. Slowly, a luminous pillar of swirling green mist came into the room and settled at the bottom of her bed. Transfixed by the apparition, she lay motionless and speechless, her mouth dry with fear. Then she heard a voice, seemingly coming from the pillar.

*"Don't be afraid. It's only Granddad. You're going to be all right, pet."*

She fell into a deep, dreamless, refreshing sleep. When she woke, the sunlight was streaming through the bedroom window and her mother was leaving for work, calling to her to get up. For the first time in months it took little effort for her to get out of bed. However, she did not go to school as she had planned. Instead, she went to her grandmother's house. Her great aunt came while she was there. Sally had not seen her niece since Christmas, and Amy's appearance worried her.

*"What on earth is the matter with that girl?"* she demanded.

*"Tonsillitis,"* replied her sister, but as she spoke, she realised how much her granddaughter had deteriorated in the few days since she had last seen her. Then defensively, she added, *"Her mother has had her to the doctor. He says it's Tonsillitis."*

*"Tonsillitis? That child has more than any Tonsillitis. If she hasn't got T.B., I'll stand tapping down the Town."*

The grandmother caught her breath, and her hand went to her mouth. Seeing the child through her sister's eyes, she was dismayed and ashamed that she had not realised the seriousness of her granddaughter's condition. Perhaps she had suspected this may be the case all along, but had been afraid even to think the name of the dreaded disease in case her thoughts made it real.

*"I'll make sure she sees the doctor tonight, even if I have to take her myself,"* she said.

The family doctor had returned from holiday and when he examined the girl his face was grave.

*"Take her straight to the chest clinic,"* he said, handing a note he had written to the mother. *"She needs an x-ray."*

Within twenty four hours the girl was admitted to the General Hospital. She was suffering from military tuberculosis. Tucked up in a hospital bed, her illness confirmed, she felt vindicated. Nobody told her the nature of her illness, but she did not care what was wrong with her as long as everyone knew that she was not lazy, and she had not invented her illness. They would have to believe her now! For the first time in months she could relax, and, best of all, she did not have to get out of bed.

Her first night in hospital was broken when she woke up in a pool of sweat and urine. She had wet the bed again! Horrified and ashamed, she lay trembling, waiting to be discovered and punished. Now and then a sob escaped, despite her attempts to muffle them in her pillow. Alerted by this, the night nurse investigated, and saw that her condition had deteriorated. He called a doctor, and without delay, they took her into the treatment room, where she had a lumbar puncture to drain fluid from her spine.

She lay absolutely still, her head between her knees, as they rubbed her spine with ether before inserting the needle. Invisible hands seemed to hold her: it was as if she realised she had to be still to allow the doctor to complete his task.

After two weeks the hospital transferred her to a children's sanatorium, where they treated her without much success for two months. She weighed only four and a half stones (63lbs) when they admitted her to the sanatorium. Part of her treatment was strict rest, which meant that she was not allowed to get out of bed for any reason. This loss of freedom did not bother her, for she had no desire to get up: she only wanted to sleep. By now she knew that she had tuberculosis, but it did not seem such a terrible disease any more.

The sanatorium was understaffed, partly due to its remote location, and overworked nurses sometimes had to bend the rules in order to get through their workload. One junior night nurse began getting the children up to go to the toilet in the morning in order to save the time taken up with her bedpan round. One morning the girl vomited in the toilet.

After that she became very ill, slipping in and out of consciousness, only vaguely aware of her surroundings. Sometimes she woke to find the staff nurse, a big, efficient, caring woman, at her bedside with a welcome drink. Her family was allowed to visit outside of the normal visiting ours, and one day her aunt Violet, her mother's sister, came to see her. Violet had always had a soft spot for her niece, and her heart sank when she saw that the child was fading away almost to nothing.

*"She's asleep,"* the sister told her when she arrived. *"She probably won't wake up while you're here."*

Violet sat beside the bed, holding her niece's frail hand, thinking that this could be the last time she would see her alive. Then the girl opened her eyes and smiled.

*"Don't cry, Auntie Violet,"* she said, *"I'm not going to die. My Granddad's been to see me, and he says I'm going to get better."*

That night the girl was transferred to the General Hospital in a critical condition. The hospital sent letters to both her parents because they feared she would die. The doctor diagnosed tubercular meningitis. She received another two lumbar punctures, but was unaware of them, for she was so weak.

As she lay in the side ward, the girl could hear her relatives talking to the staff. They spoke as if she was already dead, using the past tense when they referred to her. She did not care, as long as she did not have to get out of bed. Her Granddad had told her she was going to get better, and she believed him. Dying was something that happened to old people and to soldiers, like her Granddad during the war.

Days melted into each other: visitors were like shadows in her dreams. Occasionally, something penetrated her reverie, imprinting a memory that she would always cherish: like when her father came to see her, bringing a box of chocolates with 'MILK' written in milk bottles on the box. She was the centre of attention for the first time in her short life and it felt good.

She made a complete recovery and within ten months was discharged from hospital. She had been a model patient: her positive attitude and belief that she would recover shortened her stay at the sanatorium to a fraction of the time expected with the disease and complications she had suffered.

She returned to her life in the slums, back to school to pick up the threads of her studies and forgot about her grandfather's visit to her bedroom. She pushed it into the back of her mind as she got on with her life. There it remained, stored in her subconscious mind until something happened many years later which made her recall it.

What brought about this miraculous cure? Why did she survive while so many others succumbed to the scourge of tuberculosis? Was she, as most people believed, one of the first successes of the new 'miracle' drug, streptomycin? Undoubtedly, without the drug, and the dedicated nursing she received during her illness, she would not have survived. Yet was this enough?

Was her contact with the spirit of her grandfather a result of hallucination induced by her illness, or did he really come to help her? There have been many other recorded cases where such visions have effected or contributed to a cure. There is no doubt that her positive attitude, combined with an unshakable belief that she would recover, must have helped. Perhaps there is a time for all of us when we must die and this had not been hers. We must not forget that at this time streptomycin was a breakthrough in treating the illness, but it had not been successful in all cases. Some died despite taking the drug. Was her recovery due entirely to medical science, or was the intervention of her grandfather's spirit the factor that tipped the balance in her favour?

It could be that, by the time her illness was diagnosed, she had deteriorated to such a degree that drugs and nursing alone could not save her. Nobody, including the nursing staff and doctors who treated her, believed that she would survive. Patients whose illness was not as advanced as hers had died, so what altered the odds in her favour? Could it be that her grandfather, who had died in the

Second World War, brought healing from a spirit world? Did he hold her while the doctor drained fluid from her spine? Did he influence her behaviour, helping to speed her recovery? Did he bring healing and courage when she needed it most? The vision came at a crucial point in her illness. Perhaps without it she would not have had the energy to visit her grandmother, consequently delaying her second visit to the doctor. Every day her illness remained undiagnosed and untreated must have lessened her chances of survival.

There have been many reports throughout history which chronicle such 'miracle' cures. Alternative therapies, including spiritual healing, are becoming more popular as aids to conventional medicine. There must be a reason for this. If they did not work, the therapists would soon run out of patients.

As the narrator of this tale I can guarantee that every word of it is true. Nothing is exaggerated; the truth has not been varnished to make it more dramatic. Sometimes, when a story is handed down and retold over a period of time, a little of the truth gets lost in each telling as the narrator attempts to make it more interesting. The listener only repeats his version of what he has heard, and a dozen people listening to the same tale will each have heard it differently. Few will interpret it exactly the way the narrator intended and the story is adulterated as the listener, consciously or subconsciously, changes the original to his own interpretation.

I can assure you that I have added or changed nothing: the events were exactly as I have described. I have misinterpreted nothing, because nobody told me this story. I have known the girl, Amy, all her life and I lived through every moment with her.

# Chapter One

The working class environment in which she spent her childhood and early part of her adult life was hardly the place to inspire a passion for horses, but Amy had an overpowering obsession with them. The older members of her family thought that she was strange: she was certainly different. Who on earth did she take after? Nobody from their side of the family, that was certain. None of their relatives were strange. They could not understand how this obsession had come about and shook their heads as she cantered, whinnying, up the street on an errand. She was always a skinny little girl and nothing she wore ever fitted her. Even as the eldest, she rarely got new clothes and everything she wore started out being too big for her, so that she would grow into them. Her clothes hung from her spare frame, rather like a clothes peg doll. This, along with her behaviour, made her a comical sight.

She never walked or ran like other children, but trotted and cantered, whinnying and snorting, everywhere. Even when she was standing, she was never still, but appeared to be reining in her prancing steed. As soon as she left the house, she mounted her invisible horse and rode to wherever she was going, dismounting when she arrived, taking great care to tie her horse securely to the nearest drainpipe. Some children have invisible friends whom they talk to and play with when they are alone, but Amy never spoke of one. Perhaps her friend came in the shape of a horse.

This love of horses ruled her life. She always managed to include one in any picture she was instructed to paint in her art class at school, no matter what the subject. Street scenes included a horse and cart, while a day at the beach featured pony rides. She raided the public library for books about riding, reading them from cover to cover. If she was playing outside and heard a horse trotting along the main road, she ran to the end of her street and stood there, breathless, just to catch a glimpse of it as it passed. She had to see if it had thick legs, like a carthorse, or was a finer pony, suitable for riding, all the time dreaming of the day when she would have one of her own.

The arm of her mother's bed settee became Amy's trusty steed and she made a pair of stirrups from window cord and wire coat hangers to drape over it while she practiced her riding skills. This drove her mother to distraction, for she could not understand Amy's need to do this. She thought her daughter's behaviour strange, even unnatural. Consequently, Amy got many a cuff round the ear for riding the settee. Perhaps the mother thought that, by discouraging this behaviour, her daughter would become 'normal'. Amy knew that she would never stop loving horses, and failed to see anything unnatural in riding the settee. Where else could she practice?

When she was ill in hospital and not expected to recover, her mother promised her that she could have a pony when she got better. Perhaps she thought that it would be better to let her daughter think she could have a real pony, making what seemed to be her deathbed wish come true. However, Amy always had a knack of doing her own thing, and she did not die. Perhaps the thought of owning a pony had something to do with this and as she fought her way back to health she read even more about stable management and riding. She reasoned that, as her family knew nothing about horses, it was up to her to know how to choose the right animal and how to take care of it.

Soon, a picture of her ideal pony formed in her mind. It would be thirteen two hands high, have a large, kind eye, no vices and be as fast as the wind. This pony filled her thoughts during the day and her dreams at night.

She was in hospital for almost a year and when she returned home she eagerly looked forward to her mother purchasing the pony, but it never happened. Nobody even mentioned it. After some weeks, she plucked up the courage to ask her mother when it would be coming. Scornfully, her mother replied that 'our sort of people don't have ponies', and told Amy not to be so daft. She might be the clever one in the family, but she had no common sense.

Amy's request for her promised pony was the source of much amusement in the family, strengthening their opinion that she was 'odd'. Where did she think she could keep it? In the coal house? Or perhaps, in the outside lavatory? If she had not been wrapped up in her dream world, believing everything that adults said, Amy would have realised that, as a one parent family, her mother found difficulty in feeding her family, much less a pony. She had rent arrears, and the children got free school meals. Did Amy expect to get free food for a pony, too?

Her dreams shattered, she should, as she was almost fourteen, have come down to earth. She was nearly old enough to get a job, (at that time the school leaving age was fifteen.) so should be acting more like an adult. Instead, she consoled herself by making a stable full of cardboard horses, which she played with for hours. She had also developed a fascination for Native Americans and made headbands with strips of paper. She took great care in the design of these, for she believed that each symbol had a meaning. Fortunately, she had acquired the sense not to allow her mother see her wearing them. She already thought there was something wrong with her daughter.

That summer Amy walked the couple of miles to a riding school and asked if she could help with the horses. The owner, a bandy legged, weather beaten Irishman, gave her an unpaid job for the summer holidays. Amy was ecstatic. She did not care that she could not afford to ride the ponies. Being near them was enough for her. She felt she had finally come home, as if she belonged in a world that smelled of horses and saddle soap.

Every day during the school holidays, and at weekends throughout the summer, Amy worked in the stables. It was a long walk from her home, uphill all the way there, but there were horses to be groomed and mucked out and that was all she cared about. Now and then she had a penny, which she saved for a bus ride home, when she was tired. Part of her job was to get horses and ponies ready for the children whose parents could afford to pay five shillings for riding lessons. She had to hold the pony while the rider mounted, then go for the next one. One day, as she led the last pony out, she looked for the rider, but could not see one.

*"Don't stand there. You're making the yard untidy."* Danny, the owner said, in his thick Irish brogue. *"Get on the horse. They're leaving you behind."*

Speechless with excitement and delight, she mounted the pony and trotted after the others. Although she had never sat on a pony before, her years of practice on the arm of the settee paid dividends as she rose to the trot and caught up.

She worked all that summer and every weekend during the winter, gaining experience and perfecting her riding skills. By the end of the following summer she was dreading the thought of going back to school. The day after she received her GCE results she saw a job with horses advertised in the local paper.

*"Ring them up. I'll give you a reference,"* said Danny. *"Here. Use my telephone."*

To her surprise, Amy got the job. It meant that she would have to live away from home, but that was no hardship. At least she would have her own room, instead of having to share the bed settee with her mother, which she had done since she came out of hospital. Any desire to further her academic education was cast aside and she wrote to her headmistress, informing her that she would not be coming back.

The work was hard and for the first few weeks she found it very tiring. She had one half day off a week, which did not start until all her horses were groomed and exercised. For this she received the princely sum of three pounds a week. After deductions for National Insurance contributions and her board, she was left with sixteen shillings and nine pence. The cost of travelling home on her half day off left her with ten shillings, which she saved. She was not used to having money: it was not important to her. As long as she was working with horses, she was happy.

Unfortunately, her mother did not see things the way she did and wanted her to return home. She should look for a 'proper' job where she would not be wasting her education and at the same time contributing to the family's income. Hadn't she struggled to keep her at school until she was sixteen, so she could have a good education, and make something of her life? Wasn't it time she thought about repaying her mother for the sacrifices she had made?

Amy could have possibly resisted her mother if she had been alone in her demands, but every adult member of the family was enlisted to try to talk sense into the girl. They all agreed that she should take a job more fitting to her education, one where she could live at home. With great reluctance, Amy returned home and started work in a shipping office.

One thing she would not sacrifice was her riding. She rode once a week as a paying customer at Danny's. This fuelled the family's opinion that she was not 'normal'. 'Normal' girls of her age spent their money on nylons and makeup. Then, at seventeen, the family breathed a sigh of relief when she started courting. Other than Harry, whom she had gone to junior school with and who had singled her out as his childhood sweetheart when she came out of hospital, she had shown no interest in boys. Theirs had been a chaste, innocent relationship which lasted until her seventeenth birthday. Perhaps now that she had a 'proper' boyfriend, she would put childish things like horse riding behind her.

When we next pick up Amy's story she was happily living with Geoff, who was to be her life partner, their daughter, Susan, and Amy's daughter, Teresa. Amy's first marriage had ended in divorce after seven years. Geoff was an antique dealer and Amy helped him with the business. They were a good team and consequently made a good living. Enough to make her life's wish come true.

If Amy had stopped at one horse, perhaps her whole life might have taken a completely different turn. She had Brigadier, a fifteen hands part bred cob, Glory, a fifteen two bay Anglo-Arab mare and Little Maverick, a palomino eleven hands welsh pony. Then one day Geoff called her out to see some furniture, which Stuart, a friend from the Lake District, wanted to sell. The furniture was crammed into a double horse trailer. While Amy was trying to look at it, she heard something move. Stuart laughed at her startled expression.

*"I thought you might want to look at this little lad,"* he said. *"He's cheap, a hundred pounds with his cart and harness thrown in."*

Amy opened the groom's door at the side of the trailer and saw a large, anxious eye staring back at her. A black velvet nose blew steam towards her, and she realised that there was a Shetland pony in the space at the front of the trailer. The pony, Bobby, joined the family. Now there were four. One more mouth to feed: one more stable to muck out and because Teresa was at school, Amy had to do the work herself.

*"I need you at the shop,"* Geoff said one day. *"I have to look at some furniture this morning and there's a buyer coming this afternoon."*

*"I'll come as soon as I've finished the horses."*

*"Whether you've finished them or not, I need you to be at the shop by ten,"* he said, in the quiet way which meant that the business came before the horses.

This scene was repeated many times during the following months and it became obvious that, because there was no grazing available in the immediate area, which would cut down the need for mucking out and exercising, they needed to find a house with stables and land. But where could they find such a place? Properties with land were like gold dust, with fifty buyers for every one. They searched, applied for tenancies, but were always the under bidder, whether to buy or rent.

Then Geoff went to a smallholding on the outskirts of town. The tenant had died, and the family wanted to sell the contents of the house. He obtained the address of the landlord, who agreed to let the property to him on condition that he did the necessary repairs. On Christmas Eve, Geoff returned with the keys to the property.

The house was in poor condition and the land was littered with rubble, but it had farm buildings which could be converted into stables. Once the land was cleared and fenced it would be ideal.

There were two large bedrooms at the front of the house and two bedrooms, with sloping roofs, at the back. Teresa took one of the front bedrooms, Geoff and Amy took the other and Susan took one of the small rooms. It seemed to be their ideal home, and they were very happy, until Susan asked if she could share Teresa's room.

*"Why?"* asked Amy. *"I thought you loved your Paddington Bear room."*

*"I don't like it. It's not nice any more."*

There was ten years difference in the two sisters' ages, and it seemed a shame to make Teresa, who was seventeen, share a room with her seven-year-old sister when there were other rooms lying empty.

*"We'll have to see what Teresa thinks,"* said Geoff.

To their surprise, Teresa did not object. *"I'm amazed she hasn't moved out sooner," she said. "It's an awful room. It's spooky."*

Shortly after Susan moved in with Teresa, Amy noticed that there was something not quite right in the back bedroom. Whenever she passed the door, which was always ajar, she felt that someone was watching her and she often saw movement within the room out of the corner of her eye. When she investigated, there was nothing there. She blamed a trick of the light, but at the same time, she kept closing the door, and never went in. Teresa mentioned that she had experienced the same feelings about the room and eventually Susan admitted that she had been afraid to sleep in there. Geoff thought it was funny. Amy had always been a little weird: now the girls were going the same way.

The smallholding soon began to take shape and Amy seemed to

be determined to populate it with animals. First she bought a goat, Victoria, then some chickens, lambs, calves, ducks, geese, and, of course, three more ponies. Because goats are herd animals, Amy felt that Victoria needed company, so she bought Edward and Louisa, twin kids from the local farmers' auction mart.

Although the house was only accessible by a road leading through a field, or from a footpath at the other side of the property, Amy frequently found people in her stable yard who were under the impression that it was a riding school. Owning seven horses seemed normal to her, and she had not thought that others might be misled. There were two large, busy caravan sites within a mile of the smallholding and an idea grew in her mind. She discussed it with Geoff.

*"It wouldn't be a bad idea,"* he said. *"It would diversify. The antiques give us a good living, but you never know when the supply will dry up, or the buyers, for that matter. You know what they say about having all your eggs in one basket"*

The bank manager also thought the riding school made good business sense and was prepared to give Amy a loan to buy more horses and equipment. She obtained a licence from the local authority, sold up most of the calves and lambs, advertised and was in business.

Horses attract girls the way honey attracts bees. Soon, Amy was fully booked with lessons and rides and was inundated with offers from women and girls who wanted to help in the stables. Because she knew how they felt and understood their need to be near horses, she was sympathetic and gave them free rides whenever possible. Unfortunately, some of them looked upon her empathy as a weakness and her generosity was abused on more than one occasion.

Soon there was a nucleus of horse mad, dedicated schoolgirls between twelve and sixteen years old who spent every spare moment at the riding school. Some of them began to spend the night and it was not long before they too, began to complain about the back bedroom. Although nobody had ever actually seen a ghost, it was generally agreed that the phantom occupant of the room was the spirit of an elderly man. As the 'ghost' did not seem to want to leave the room, Geoff locked the door and forbade anyone to use it.

Amy tried to discourage the girls from talking about the old man in case it upset some of the younger customers. However, now and then, a new mum would ask about the ghost, so it was a very difficult secret to keep.

The riding school flourished and the number of horses and ponies grew to more than twenty. Then Geoff began to act strangely. He had constant headaches, often lost his temper and was rude to customers. Finally, Amy managed to persuade him to see a doctor, who diagnosed migraine. Amy was sure that it was something more serious, and she was right. Two days after seeing the doctor Geoff collapsed. He was taken to hospital, where he had a successful operation for a benign brain tumour.

It was many months before Geoff could work again, so they had to close the antiques business. Now the riding school became their only source of income and Amy had to come up with ways of earning enough money to pay the bills. When looking through a pony magazine belonging to one of the helpers, she saw advertisements for children's riding holidays.

By this time, the back bedroom had become a junk room, but Amy cleared it out and decorated it so that it was bright and cheerful. She found some wallpaper with a pattern depicting scenes from the Horse of the Year Show, and everyone agreed that it looked good when it was finished. Soon they were ready for the first guests.

The girls were sworn to secrecy. Anyone heard discussing the occupant of the back bedroom would be banished from the stables. Still, Amy had an anxious first week, fully expecting the two girls who shared the Horse of the Year Show room, as it became known, to complain. They did not, and when they left they thanked her for a wonderful holiday.

The weeks went by and more children occupied the Horse of

the Year Show room without incident. Amy began to think that the old man had left, or that they had all imagined him: until she was woken in the middle of the night by screams of terror.

She reached the bedroom first and found one of its young occupants trembling with fear. The girl claimed that she had seen a man by the bedroom door and, as she described him, Amy knew that the girl had seen the old man. Amy sat with her until both girls were asleep, then went back to bed herself, leaving the back bedroom door open. The rest of the night passed without incident and the explanation she gave her other guests the next morning was that the girl had had a nightmare. After that she took no more bookings that would necessitate someone sleeping in the Horse of the Year Show room.

The only other time the room was occupied after that was by the son of a family friend, a lad of fifteen. His family had moved to a nearby town from a rural area and he was homesick. Jim loved coming to the stables, where he could be near the horses and other animals, and was grateful when Amy said he could stay during the school holidays.

As time went by they noticed that Jim was reluctant to go to bed and regularly fell asleep downstairs. Like Susan, he refused to close the bedroom door. It must have taken a lot of courage to go back to that room every night, and his pride prevented him from admitting that there was a problem. Jim's family moved back to Norfolk a few months later, and he never spoke about what made him so reluctant to go to bed. After that, Geoff closed the door tightly, and they did not use the room again.

Familiarity breeds contempt and through time the family became so used to the old man that nobody mentioned him. The old man became very quiet, too. Was this because he was not being disturbed? Or did nobody bother him because he was being so quiet? Whatever the reason, it suited the family just fine.

It never occurred to them that they should get rid of him. They had learned to share the house with him amicably. As far as Amy was concerned, he cost nothing to keep and now seemed to be house trained. She was a firm believer in leaving well alone and she did not wish to know why the spirit of the old man had chosen to live in her back bedroom. She had no use for the room, so, as long as he behaved himself and followed the rules of the house, he was welcome to stay as long as he wished.

Many people have had similar experiences and not many of them would have reacted the way Amy did. Some would have investigated further, determined to know all about this lost soul. Others might accept nothing less than the exorcism of the spirit. Religious beliefs create a formidable barrier for some. So many religions frown on the idea of communicating with the 'dead', pointing out that it says in the bible that you should not consult mediums. However, they will also say that the only way to Heaven is through their own particular religion, which Amy always found hard to accept. She felt that there are as many paths to God as there are people on Earth, and if one religion fails to inspire you, then you should try another until you find one which sits easily on your shoulders.

This is not intended to be a detailed biography, but an account of how Amy discovered that she was mediumistic and of her subsequent development as a person and a Spiritualist medium. This metamorphosis was gradual, and occurred over a period of years: sometimes the changes were dramatic, other times they were almost unnoticeable. Amy discovered, through this journey, that Spiritualism is a way of life and as she began to live according to its teachings, she discovered her true self.

Many mediums appear to have always been able to see and communicate with spirits from an early age. There must also have been others who have had this ability, but chose to suppress it because they did not wish to appear 'different'. They build a barrier between themselves and spirit communicators until they are no longer aware of them. The reasons for doing this are many. They may have realised that their ability to see or hear spirits was not shared by their peers. Not wishing to be regarded as an oddity, or perhaps, because of strict religious taboos, they may be afraid of being treated for mental instability, so learn to be discreet about visitors only they are aware of.

Not all Spiritualists are born into Spiritualism. Most are brought up in 'orthodox' religions, and find their way to Spiritualism for a wide variety of reasons. The most common reason is the need to know that a loved one's spirit really has just 'passed on', and has survived physical death. Others, like Amy, have experiences, and need to know how to handle them. Some of these go on to become Spiritualist mediums, others exploit their new found psychic awareness, and, sadly, others seek help elsewhere, and continue to be dismayed at the thought of having unseen etheric bodies as their constant companions.

Why was Amy chosen to work as a medium? What special attributes did she have? There does not seem to be any blueprint for a typical medium: they come from all walks of life. Some are educated and articulate: a great asset and an essential qualification for mediumship, which is based on communication. However, there is always the exception which proves the rule, and through the years, many excellent mediums have had little formal education.

Everyone has some degree of inherited psychic abilities, and these are stronger in those who are mediumistic. As she learned more, Amy was to discover that psychic ability alone is not enough on its own to make a medium. Fortunately, she was already an ethical and caring person, but she needed to develop these qualities and learn to control her gift.

Amy has had many ambitions at various stages of her life, some of which she managed to fulfil. Becoming a Spiritualist medium was never one of these: it never entered her mind. Her world revolved around her family, her business and her animals. If anyone had suggested to her that one day she would devote her Sunday evenings to travelling around Spiritualist churches taking services, she would have laughed in their faces. But that was before things began to go bump in the night.......

# Chapter Two

Amy snuggled next to Geoff and patted the side of the bed. Tim, her Jack Russell terrier, jumped up, tail wagging, and settled down beside her. He licked her hand to say thank you and goodnight. It had been a long day: she lay for a while, trying to relax, dismissing her thoughts in preparation for sleep. Then she began to feel uneasy. What was wrong? What was this strange feeling, a tangible, invisible vibration of energy, which reach out and touched her?

Her first thought was that the old man had decided to leave his room and was paying her a visit. Ghosts have no physical form, so they can go through walls and closed doors. If it was the old man, why had he suddenly decided to leave 'his' room? She had never actually been afraid of him, but had always given him a wide berth, working on the principle that, if she did not bother him he would not bother her. They had shared the same house for eight years now, and he had never left 'his' room to her knowledge. Then she realised that it did not feel like him. Whoever stood beside her bed was someone she had never known before. Why was he here? (She had no idea whether he was male or female, but referred to him in her mind as 'he'.)

With a startled whimper, Tim dived under the duvet and disappeared down to the bottom of the bed. There he lay, trembling and whining softly. This was totally out of character, for Tim was a courageous little dog, whose job it was to keep down rats and other vermin on the property. He was usually too brave for his own good and afraid of nothing.

Geoff snored gently, and she snuggled closer to him, hugging his broad, warm back for comfort. How could he sleep when she was so afraid? She tried to wake him up, but she could not make her body do what her mind was telling it. Geoff's nearness made her feel braver, but not enough to look to see who was standing there, waiting for her to acknowledge his presence.

Then, without warning, the presence was gone. She did not look to her side to check he was no longer there. She just knew it. Besides, Tim came back up the bed, sheepishly wagging his stump of a tail. Amy cuddled him. He licked her hand and they fell asleep, comfortable in each other's presence.

The next day Amy decided not to tell Geoff about her experience. He would have treated it as a joke and accused her of dreaming it. In the cold light of day, she wondered if she had imagined it, but if that was the case, Tim had imagined it too. Perhaps it was a dream: a realistic nightmare. She decided to keep her own counsel and to try to forget what had happened.

The hard physical work which she did in the riding school kept her busy all day and by bedtime she was very tired. Geoff was already asleep when she and Tim climbed into bed. She knew that her visitor had returned when Tim, hackles bristling, began to shake and growl. Before he could desert her, she grabbed him and held him close for comfort and protection. He began to pant, wriggling frantically in an effort to free himself, scratching her neck in the process. He was becoming distressed, so she let him go. He promptly bolted to his refuge at the bottom of the bed. She could feel him trembling, his nose hot and wet against her feet.

Her courage disappeared down the bed with her dog, and she felt defenceless without him. Wrapping herself up in the duvet, she closed her eyes tightly, and clung to Geoff until the presence had gone.

The next morning she thought over what had happened, exploring the possible explanations. She felt she needed to confide in someone, but what would she say? That someone was standing by her bed at night? Someone who did not speak and whom she was afraid to look at? It did not sound logical and they would say she had imagined it, or blame it on the 'change'. She had not started the menopause and she knew that the presence was real, not imagined. After all, Tim had experienced it too: he was not menopausal and terriers are not renowned for their powers of imagination, other than their conviction that they are invincible.

The presence continued to visit Amy for another four months. Each night she turned her back to him and waited for him to go, unable to sleep until he had done so. By this time the fearless Tim had thrown in the towel and was sleeping on the settee in the living room.

After a while, Amy noticed that her wedding ring began to feel unbearably tight just before the presence arrived. This was strange, because she had begun to lose weight, something she had tried unsuccessfully to do for years. Her nightdress also felt tight, as if it was too small for her, when in fact it was now a size too big. She began to think that perhaps she was starting the menopause, but the intense, dry heat, which seared through her, starting deep inside her chest, was entirely different from the hot, damp flushes of menopause which she experienced four years later. This dry heat did not come and go as her later flushes did: it remained constant.

As she lay awake, she began to think of people she had lost contact with, most of whom she had not seen or heard from in twenty five years. Night after night they came into her mind, rekindling a past she had almost forgotten. Among these were memories of a long lost love. These memories obsessed her to the extent that she could not stop talking about an ex boyfriend, Ivan. He was a handsome Hungarian refugee who had broken her heart when she had been eighteen years old. The pain she had suffered when he left her: the emptiness as she learned to live without the man with whom she had girlishly imagined that she would spend the rest of her life, returned to her. She felt she had to know what had happened to him, but to do that she would have to find him. She tried looking at public records, to no avail.

Then she tried every regional telephone book in the country, but he was not listed. How could he have vanished without a trace? Was he trying to contact her now? If so, why had he picked this time to get in touch? Where was he? Was he dead? If not, what had he to do with the presence at her bedside?

All these questions remained unanswered. She did not understand what was happening and had no idea where to go to find out. Yet at the back of her mind there was a feeling that she should be looking for something. Ivan was just a small part of it.

By now she had lost almost three stones in weight. She had been on a diet and, for the first time in many years, it was working. She became more active and felt better. Instead of waving goodbye to the rides, she began accompanying them, enjoying riding once again. Her morale rose as she watched the weight fall away and she felt that she was more capable of dealing with problems. Even her visitor did not frighten her any more. He was part of her routine and she waited until he left before she went to sleep. Then one night, as she waited for him to go, she felt the side of the duvet rise up. Alarmed, she called out, in her mind, "Please, go away!"

He left immediately. She was amazed and could not believe how simple it had been. She had only needed to ask him to go. She was later to realise that asking the spirit to go was her first conscious communication with the spirit world. As she learned more, she began to regret her ignorance and fear that night. The presence had felt so strong that had she investigated, instead of retreating under the duvet, she might have discovered who her visitor was. She has never discovered his identity and now regrets that her first conscious communication with a spirit friend was to ask him to go.

She waited for him the following night but he did not come. She hardly slept, expecting to feel him there, but there was no sign of him. Now that he was gone, she missed him and wondered if he had ever meant to frighten her. She realised by now that he had not intended her any harm and had never been a threat. She had frightened herself because of her ignorance and reluctance to discover his identity.

Now she felt ready to confide in someone. She chose Val, a married woman in her thirties, who came to the stables daily to help in the school. Val was fascinated. It was the sort of thing she enjoyed, for she was an avid reader of horror and supernatural fiction. She put forward various suggestions as to the identity of the visitor, none of which Amy felt happy with. Then she announced that one of her husband's work colleagues was a Spiritualist who held séances regularly at his home. She suggested that Amy should visit one of these.

Amy could not see herself sitting in a darkened room with a bunch of old biddies, asking *"Is anyone there?"* However, she was willing to try almost anything. So one evening, she told Geoff she was going to the cinema with Val and set off to keep her appointment with the medium.

The medium, Edna, said she was a Spiritualist. She worked from home using a small table, through which she claimed to receive messages from the spirit world. She lived with her husband, Billy, in a small red brick terraced house twenty miles away. They were a very ordinary, respectable, elderly working class couple, not at all what Amy had imagined Spiritualists to look like. There were to be only four at the séance: Edna, Bill, Amy and Val.

Edna tried to put them at ease and warned them that it was quite usual for nothing to happen at a first sitting and they should not be disappointed. She also explained that the table might rise in the air and that they might see or hear things. However, she did not explain that they should speak out if they saw or heard anything, or that they should share any experiences with the other sitters. Consequently, Amy thought that she was there to watch and listen, not to take an active part in the proceedings.

They were taken into a small front room which was overcrowded with too much furniture. There was barely enough space for the four of them to sit around the small square table. Billy closed the curtains and lit the gas fire, the only heating in the room. When they were seated around the table he turned off the light. Amy had her back to the fire, which began to splutter as soon as she sat down. Edna was on Amy's right, Billy on her left and Val sat opposite. Nobody mentioned, or attempted to adjust the gas fire, so Amy thought it best to ignore it. They began by singing a popular hymn, then Edna said a short prayer, after which they all said the Lord's Prayer.

*"Hold hands,"* said Edna. They sat for a few minutes like this then she told them to relax and place their hands gently on the table and sit quietly. Not sure where to look, Amy fixed her eyes on Val's hands and as she watched, they grew longer and became finer. They shimmered luminously in the dim light, glowing pure white. She lifted her eyes, intending to draw Val's attention to what was happening to her hands, but she had disappeared. In her place, there was a monk, at least twice her size. Amy was not afraid of this monk, nor was she surprised to see him. She assumed that this was what happened at séances. It did not occur to her to announce that she could see him: she assumed that the others could see him too. His cowl cast a shadow over his face, obscuring it from her view, but she could clearly make out the thick, course material of his brown habit.

Her wedding ring began to feel tight, so she slipped it into her pocket. Then she averted her gaze away from the monk and looked at the wall above him. It appeared to be covered in a thick dark grey-brown smoke. There was an opening in the smoke, like the entrance of a cave. The inside of this 'cave' was very bright and she could see people moving about inside. Now and then one of them appeared at the entrance, as if presenting themselves to be recognised. One girl in particular seemed to loiter at the 'cave' entrance. She looked as though she was in her late twenties and had shoulder length, heavy blonde hair which she flicked occasionally with her hand.

Amy did not realise at the time that she should have shared her experiences with the others: she should have announced that she could see the monk and described the people who came to the cave entrance. Someone may have recognised the spirits who had come forward to be recognised. Because she did not fully understand what was happening, they all missed the opportunity to communicate with these spirits.

*"Put your hands lightly on the table, fingers touching the person's hands next to you,"* said Edna. *"I can feel a lady coming close. I feel that she is for Amy. She was a striking looking woman, about five foot seven, her clothes are old fashioned, probably from the early fifties, and she lived in Yorkshire."*

*"I'm sorry, I don't recognise her."* said Amy.

*"What about you, Val?"* asked Edna.

*"No, I don't, either."*

Val had returned to Amy's view once more, and seemed at ease with what was happening. Amy was tempted to catch her eye, to tell her about the monk, then thought it would be prudent to wait until after the séance.

Just then the table began to wobble, then it rose into the air until all four legs were off the ground. Slowly, it began to move in a swinging motion. Amy was not worried. Billy had warned them that the table might do this.

*"I'm going to ask some questions and the table will spell out the answers,"* said Edna, *"and I've still got that woman with me. Are you sure you don't recognise her, Amy?"*

Amy shook her head. *"No,"* she said, *"I don't know anybody who lived in Yorkshire."*

*"Never mind. She might come to you later,"* said Billy.

As the séance continued, various emotions washed over Amy, particularly disappointment and frustration. At one point she felt weighed down with sadness, almost despair, and tears flowed freely from her eyes, soaking her lap, even though she was not crying. She knew that they were not her feelings. She just seemed to be witnessing them.

*"I feel that somebody's trying to come through, and is frustrated because he or she is not being recognised,"* she said, amazed that she had the courage to speak.

*"Maybe the spirit wants to speak through Amy."* suggested Billy.

*"Do you want to speak through Amy?"* Edna said to the table. It moved, signifying that it did.

This was foolish and very irresponsible of the medium and her husband to allow this to happen. How could they expect Amy, without training or experience, to be successful where the medium had failed? They were exposing her to something that she was not equipped to handle, and as experienced sitters, they should have known this.

However, fools rush in and Amy was no exception. She was a little flattered to think that she could succeed where the medium had failed. Nevertheless, there is no substitute for experience. She commenced by asking naïve questions, most of which would have required more than a yes or no answer. Not surprisingly, she was unsuccessful and Edna took charge once again.

*"Could you please spell out your name."* she said.

The table moved its way through the alphabet until it reached the letter 'I'. The tears in Amy's eyes were her own this time, as she realised that Ivan was probably dead and it was his spirit who was attempting to communicate with them. Then, as the table began its journey through the alphabet, it began to wobble, as if resisting some force that was trying to manoeuvre it. By now Amy was upset. She was convinced that Ivan was trying to communicate with her and that someone was manipulating the table, thus preventing him from doing so. Then she noticed that Edna seemed to be moving her hands, using pressure to try to spell out a different name. Edna asked the table to start again and it again stopped at the letter 'I'. Then, as it continued, Amy saw that Edna was anticipating another name and was trying to manipulate the table accordingly.

A cold rage swept over Amy. As before, the rage was not her own and although she experienced it, she was perfectly calm in herself. Then she felt the table melt beneath her fingers: its surface felt as if it was made of soft toffee. A sense of power surged through her and she felt as if she could plunge her fingers into the soft surface and stop the table. This she did. She could not allow this woman to mock the spirit who had come forward to be recognised.

That night Amy was used as a channel by someone she did not recognise or understand. As her fingers sank into the table, she felt herself pressing them firmly down, causing the table to stop. Three loud raps came from underneath the table. Then there was silence. Billy jumped up and turned on the light. Throughout the séance, for reasons she did not know, Amy had avoided looking at Billy, although she was aware of a glow coming from him.

They moved into the living room and Amy was surprised to see that they had been sitting for more than an hour and a half. Billy made a pot of tea while the others talked.

*"I'm surprised that you did not know who that woman was that I brought for you, Amy."* said Edna. *"She was very clear and the way she was standing, it was as if she was posing for a photograph."*

Amy put her cup down, as memories of Ivan flooded back to her. He had shown her a dog eared, black and white photograph of his mother, who had married an RAF officer during the war and had moved with him to a town in Yorkshire, leaving Ivan in Hungary in the care of his grandmother. Amy felt as if she had been impolite and had turned away a guest. The fact that she did not recognise the woman is not surprising. Many people who visit a medium, or attend a Spiritualist church for the first time, are looking for a message from one or two particular loved ones. They concentrate on these and block their minds off to anyone who may come forward for them. It is quite natural for people to do this, for if you are mourning the loss of someone very close to you, you hardly want to speak to that person's aunt or uncle, whom you hardly knew. You feel that they are pushing in, keeping the one you seek away from you. Amy was so confident that she would hear from Ivan that she resisted any other spirit who came forward.

The two friends had a lot to talk about as they drove home. Amy did most of the talking and she was surprised that Val had experienced none of the phenomena that she herself had seen.

Val had felt the table tilt and heard the raps at the end, but nothing else. What Amy found even more incredible was that Val had not realised that the monk had appeared to take her place. Val was intrigued and a little envious as Amy related her experiences.

After dropping Val off, Amy returned home and went straight to bed, half expecting her visitor to put in an appearance. He did not and she slept soundly, happy in the thought that Ivan was probably still alive: it was his mother who was trying to talk to her.

Over the years Amy was to learn that people often grasp at straws when they accept evidence from a medium and frequently shape the message to fit their circumstances. She also learned that there are people, like Edna and Billy, who are able to produce psychic phenomena, but are not worried if what they produce is genuine or partially manipulated by themselves. They do not actually manufacture the phenomena, but embellish it with their own efforts. Amy did not think that there was any fraud intended, except perhaps, for Edna's attempts to spell out the name.

They could not have faked Amy's feeling that the table top had melted; the elongation of Val's hands; the appearance of the monk, or the people Amy had seen in the 'cave'. If they had, they would have been capable of producing special effects of which Steven Spielberg would have been proud. What motive would they have had for faking it? They did not ask for any money. The sitting was free.

Amy was puzzled about why she had been aware of so much, while the others had not. She did not realise at the time that she was probably seeing the spirits clairvoyantly and this had come about because she was sitting in an atmosphere conducive to spirit activity. Had everyone seen the spirits, it would have been classed as physical phenomena, which needs ectoplasm to form materialised spirits and move the table. As the others had not seen the monk or the people in the cave, the table was probably moved by their combined psychic energies. However, the three raps at the end of the séance were heard by everyone. That indicates that they, at least, were a result of physical phenomena, and ectoplasm would have been necessary to produce them.

Val's husband promised to ask Billy what he and his wife thought about the séance. Amy could hardly wait for Tuesday, but was not prepared for what Val had to say.

*"Edna said that someone came with you to the séance,"* said Val. *"And she says he was evil."*

Amy was horrified. She had been completely calm and unafraid throughout the séance, yet now she was scared of someone she could neither see nor hear. Until Val uttered those words, Amy had felt that she had taken a step forward and was on her way to understanding what was happening to her. She had experienced nearly every emotion during the séance, with the exception of fear, but now she was very afraid. She could not bear to think that an invisible evil spirit was her constant companion, who might do harm to her or her family.

That night she went to the bedroom, changed into her nightdress, then returned downstairs. Tim was delighted to have her company and welcomed her onto the settee. She spent the next two weeks knitting, reading or playing patience until she saw the first light of dawn appear. The daylight gave her the courage to slip quietly into bed, attempting to fit a full night's sleep into three hours. Geoff did not say anything, but he must have wondered why she had begun to come to bed at four in the morning.

Then one night, as she was making a cup of tea to help her to stay awake, a thought came into her mind. At no time during the conversations she had had with Edna and Billy did they mention anything remotely connected with evil. They had shown no sign of discomfort or fear during the time she was with them and had been relaxed in her company. Then she began to wonder if they had used the word 'evil' at all. They must have known that she had been the instrument used to stop the table, and would have realised that someone had given her the power to do that. They would also know that power does not necessarily mean evil.

The more she thought about it, the more Amy realised that neither Billy nor Edna had used the word 'evil' to describe any spirit who had accompanied her to the séance. They may have used the word 'strong', or even 'powerful'. She realised that the message could have been distorted as it was relayed back to her. She put her cup down and went to bed, unafraid of the darkness and slept soundly and undisturbed.

After a good night's sleep, Amy decided that Val had the wrong attitude and it would not be in her interest to continue her search in her company. What she had suffered because of Val's thoughtlessness illustrates the misery that can be the result of careless words. Amy had been afraid to sleep in her own bed at night because Val had dramatised a situation that Amy had considered to be a serious undertaking. Amy felt that Val had twisted the medium's words to fit in with the rubbishy horror fiction of which she was so fond. She probably did not realise what she was doing, or that it would scare Amy. After all, they were supposed to be friends. Her ignorance may have excused her, but it meant that Amy could no longer trust her in this particular matter. They did not have the same priorities. She was seeking sensationalism, while Amy was seeking knowledge.

Now Amy felt frustrated. She was not quite back to square one, but she had not made a lot of progress. She had experienced such a feeling of power when the spirit had used her to stop the table. She wanted to feel that power again and to find out about this spirit world. At the same time she did not feel that she could go back to Edna's, with or without Val. After a lot of thought, she decided to continue her search, but in another direction and with a more suitable companion. It was about this time that she began to have the dreams that all came true.

# Chapter Three

Precognition is a phenomenon dating back to the beginning of man's recorded history. There are accounts of seers who were consulted before ancient rulers took decisions concerning war and other important events. In the Bible, Joseph's dreams predicted the years of plenty and famine, saving the lives of many thousands of people. Today, although man is more sophisticated and less inclined to believe that it is possible to predict the future, there are still reports of people who have dreamed about world events before they happen. These claims are often hard to prove, for it is usually only when the event occurs that the dreamer is prompted to recall his dream.

Amy began to have dreams that were both unusual and vivid. They were more like visions and she could always tell them apart from her normal dreams. She could remember all of the details of these 'vision dreams' the following morning. Family and friends became used to them, eventually ceasing to be surprised when they all came true. They already thought Amy was odd, for she regularly got up and walked to the telephone just before it rang.

It was when she began to dream the winners of horse races that her friends realised that this was more than coincidence. Because she lived outside of town, she did not have a newspaper delivered. Her television did not have a text facility, so she had no way of knowing which horses were engaged to run in the races the following day. The only thing the horses she dreamed about had in common was that they all subsequently won and they were all outsiders: their starting prices were always at least twenty five to one.

One example was a dream she had which featured a horse being led into the winners' enclosure by a female leprechaun. She told her friends and the next day Carolyn rang to say that a horse named Leprechaun Lady had won. Another coincidence? That is a possibility, but Amy's life was full of coincidences these days. When coincidences become so frequent that they are accepted as normal, one must wonder why they do happen.

She never knew when the dreams would take place, nor could she consciously make them happen or dream about a particular subject to order. If she could have done that she would have been able to forecast winners regularly, which she could not. The dreams were completely spontaneous and without a perceivable pattern.

It was not just the dreams that occurred while she was asleep. Often, when faced with a problem, she felt that she should delay actions or decisions until the following day. This is not unusual, because many people often use the phrase 'let me sleep on it'. She invariably woke up with the solution, or with new ideas that proved helpful in her business. She felt she was being guided. Perhaps she was. We are told that we all have spirit guides who are there to help us during our lives. Amy's guide had taken a back seat for most of her life, but he had always been there. She had not been aware of him, but now she sensed his presence. She was learning to listen.

She had not, as yet, chosen someone else to accompany her in her search. Once bitten, twice shy. She had to be sure not to repeat her mistake. Also, the desire to find out what was happening to her had slipped down the list of her order of priorities. The daily problems of the riding school, as it geared up towards its busiest time of year, occupied most of her waking hours. The person she eventually chose was a customer, a midwife, who frequently worked night shifts, so was often absent from the stables for long periods, depending on her shifts. She also featured in Amy's next dream, which was as follows:-

*Pauline was watching television in Amy's living room, engrossed in the horses as they paraded before a race. Amy asked her why* she was so interested in the race. Pauline replied that she had placed a bet on one of the runners. (Pauline never gambled, so this was unusual.) Amy then asked which horse she had put her money on and Pauline pointed to the horse she had chosen. Amy asked why she had chosen that particular horse and Pauline replied that she always placed a bet on horses with a tree in their name. Amy shook her head, and advised Pauline to look elsewhere for the winner.

*The race was a steeplechase and the horses raced clockwise around the track. Pauline's horse did not win: a horse whose jockey wore bright yellow colours finished first.*

Amy was bemused by the dream and was still thinking about it when she went into the town the following day. The flat racing season had started and there was very little chance of a steeplechase being televised on a Thursday in May. She was standing in the long queue (it was pension day) at the post office, when Pauline tapped her on the shoulder.

*"Get me a couple of first class stamps, will you?"* she whispered, then, louder, *"I was on my way to see you."*

Seeing Pauline brought the dream into Amy's mind again. After she was served, she told Pauline about the dream. Pauline was intrigued and eagerly accompanied Amy into the betting shop. They were greeted by the manageress.

*"There is no jump racing on the telly this afternoon, is there?"* asked Amy, shaking her head, anticipating a negative answer.

*"As it happens, there is,"* replied the manageress. *"There's only one. It's an amateur riders' race at Sandown. The rest are all flat races."*

Sandown is a right handed track, so the horses would be racing clockwise. Amy told the manageress about her dream and the three of them scanned the runners for the steeplechase. The first horse on the list was named Elmboy. It was a hot favourite to win. The dream was right so far! They began to search through the descriptions of the jockey's racing colours, looking for one with a yellow jacket. Then they saw, right at the bottom, a horse name

Yellow Jersey.

Now they really were excited. Surely the next step would be to place a bet on the horse. As they read the newspaper tipsters' views on the race, they realised that Yellow Jersey had no chance of beating Elmboy. He was an unconsidered outsider, quoted at 33-1 in the betting forecast, and on all known form he should not finish in the first dozen, let alone win.

The more they read, the more confused they were. Should they to believe the dream or the tipsters? They eventually decided to have a fifty pence reversed forecast, which meant that the two horses would have to finish first or second in either order for the bet to win. Pauline pointed out that both of the horses had been mentioned in the dream, but it would be silly to be carried away. Fifty pence each was enough to risk on a dream.

Amy made cheese and tomato on toast for them both and they ate it on plates balanced on their knees in front of the television as they watched the race. Elmboy was long odds on and looked a class above the others as he cantered to the starting gate. Then they were off. Pauline and Amy jumped up and down in excitement as the horses approached the last fence, with both Elmboy and Yellow Jersey in the first four. Yellow Jersey went on to win the race. Elmboy broke down after the last fence and finished fourth. They had lost their money. By trying to make sense of the dream they had disregarded how it had ended, with Yellow Jersey winning. I do not think that Amy was meant to profit from these glimpses into the future. The dreams were only meant to get her attention.

Once Pauline got over the disappointment of not benefiting financially from the dream, she began to take a more active interest in what was happening to Amy. Having tasted the excitement generated by the possibility that the future could be foreseen, she wanted to know more. As they discussed what the next step should be, Amy realised that she had found her new companion.

A week later, Pauline obtained the name of a psychic who read tarot cards and who came highly recommended. The psychic had premises in a nearby city and charged five pounds for a sitting.

They booked, using false names, and set of to see the psychic like a pair of overgrown, excited schoolgirls, not knowing what to expect.

The premises were in the middle of the city, up a flight of stairs and more than a little shabby. However, they were not there to admire the décor. They sat in the reception area, trying hard not to giggle, pretending that they were not apprehensive. As they waited, Amy began to feel silly. What was she doing, a woman of her age, and of reasonable intelligence, visiting a fortune teller? (And paying a fiver, too!) If this woman was really any good she would be making a lot of money and would be able to afford to redecorate her premises. Then the door opened, a woman came out and it was Amy's turn.

The psychic was younger than Amy, yet she had an air of authority which made you feel like a child. She was sitting across a desk with her back to the window, a pack of tarot cards in front of her. She invited Amy to sit down then shuffled the cards, placing some of them on the desk in front of her. Then she closed her eyes. When she opened them, she began to speak.

*"I have your father,"* she began. Her face contorted as if she was in great pain. *"He passed over in unpleasant circumstances. He was alone and in pain. I feel he was short of breath. There was no family around him when he passed over, or to mourn him at his funeral."*

Amy was astounded. She had been told only a month previously that her father had died in hospital, suffering from asbestosis. As he had been estranged from her family for many years, none of them had been informed of his illness or death. He was cremated before any of them were told of his death.

The woman went on to give Amy information about family and friends, living and dead, which was reasonably accurate. There was no way that this woman could have known anything about her, as Amy was booked in Pauline's maiden name in case the woman had some means of obtaining information about them. Later, she realised that these precautions were unnecessary, for nobody could possibly check up on all of their customers. Not when she only charged a fiver! Amy had never been to a psychic before, so was possibly keen to make things fit. Not everything the woman had said was accurate and when Amy corrected her, she altered it to fit. However, she did tell Amy something which she could not accept at the time which later proved to be true. Except for a small piece of information that could have possibly related to Ivan, Amy did not feel that the sitting had helped her in her search. The woman made her feel that her father still existed, only in another form, and that he still cared about his daughter. Amy wanted to know more about the spirit world that the woman had spoken of.

Pauline was not as impressed with the psychic as Amy had been, although she was given scraps of information that she could accept. They discussed their sittings on their way home and concluded that it had sharpened their appetite for more. Pauline had been adopted as a child, and consequently, knew very little about her natural parents, so they felt that her sitting was reasonable in the circumstances. Their next step would be to find a Spiritualist church, to see what it had to offer.

They chose a church in the same city. It would not do to be seen entering a Spiritualist meeting nearer home, for Amy was in business and Pauline was a midwife. They had to protect their reputations. Like most people who are not acquainted with Spiritualism, they did not realise that it was a religion. Consequently, they relied on what they had learned from popular fiction and were apprehensive, not sure in what strange rituals they might be expected to participate.

They did not realise that Spiritualist churches are sometimes located in houses, halls and even community centres. Because they were looking for a church building and saw groups of people entering a church on the same road as the one they were looking for, they assumed they had found the right place. It was only when they heard some of the congregation talking that they realised their mistake. Shamefaced, they had to ask directions from the good Christians, who obviously disapproved of Spiritualism. Some seemed to pity them, and prayers were probably said in the church that night for Amy and Pauline's misguided souls. Scarlet faced and unable to look anyone in the eye, they scuttled out and headed along the road to the Spiritualist church.

The directions they had been given were excellent and they were soon entering the front door of the building which housed the Spiritualist church. A woman met them and sold them some raffle tickets. The prize, a dog eared set of cheap toiletries, had probably started life as an unwanted Christmas gift before embarking on a long, debilitating but honourable career in raffles. The woman also indicated a bowl that was marked 'DONATIONS'. They were not sure how much to give, but as there seemed to be only ten and twenty pence pieces in the bowl, they thought it would be reasonable to donate fifty pence each.

The woman led them into a room where the service had started. The congregation, about a dozen in all, were singing a hymn as the two friends self consciously found their seats in the back row. When the hymn finished Amy expected that the lights would be turned off, thinking that it would be run on similar lines to the séance she had attended. To her relief, the lights remained on throughout the service.

The room was drab and Amy felt cold, despite having a warm coat on. Two men and a woman sat, facing the congregation, at the front of the room. After the hymn one of the men, who seemed to be the chairman, began to talk about Spiritualism. This talk lasted for more than twenty minutes and consisted of his experiences, often referring to people that Amy had never heard of. He frequently slotted the names of these great healers and mediums into his talk, obviously meaning to impress his audience. Amy looked around and saw that most of the congregation were as unimpressed as she was. They seemed to be waiting for him to finish, so they could get on with the rest of the service.

Pauline nudged her and indicated a trio of women in the front row who were passing boiled sweets around. Amy grimaced, feeling that this was bad manners. She shuddered. It seemed to be getting colder. She tried to listen to what the speaker was saying, but he was only repeating what he had previously told them. Then he finally brought his saga to a conclusion and sat down. They sang another hymn before the chairman announced that the mediums would start their clairvoyance. Immediately, the attitude of the congregation changed. They sat up straight, their eyes fixed on the man who had risen to his feet.

He was younger than the chairman and very pleasant in his manner. He went from one woman to another, speaking to them about their friends and loved ones who had 'passed on.' From the responses he got, Amy could see that this man was a good medium. Now she sat a little straighter, hoping to catch his eye, but he sat down without looking her way. The chairman stood up and looked towards her.

*"Can I speak to that lady at the back?"* he asked.

Reluctantly, Amy nodded and he began the message. As with the psychic, there were pieces of information which could have been correct, but most of the message was made up with vague, general information, which could have applied to many of the congregation. Now she was disappointed as well as cold.

The chairperson approached them after the service. He had recognised that this was their first visit to a Spiritualist church and attempted to give them an insight into Spiritualism. They asked him a lot of questions, in the hope that he could explain why Amy was having psychic experiences. He seemed disinterested and unimpressed in what they had to say. He wanted them to listen to what he had to say and used words that they, as lay people, did not understand. When Amy mentioned she had been to a séance, he took them to a room which he informed them was set aside for this purpose. He explained how he had seen spirits materialise in that very room. He went on to tell of tables levitating, and trumpets flying around the room, used by unseen spirits to communicate with the sitters.

They found these stories more interesting than his talk, but they were looking for answers, not more tales of phenomena. They believed that what he told them was true, but it did not help them to understand what was happening to Amy. Other people's experiences, however wonderful, do not have the same effect on the listener when recounted. They have little meaning other than to the person who experienced them first hand. Whenever Amy told him of one of her experiences, he replied with his own tales, completely unrelated to what she had said. It was as if he was competing with her for the strangest story.

They felt that they were an uninformed, captive audience, too polite to interrupt him as he had interrupted their stories. As they stood in the icy cold room, which smelled vaguely of fish, Amy felt that she was being rocked back onto her heels. Invisible hands gripped her under the armpits and she felt that someone was gently easing her out of her body. Afraid, she asked if they could go. He offered them a cup of tea, but they did not fancy listening to more of his tales. They made their excuses and left.

On the way home, they analysed their evening. Had they asked the wrong questions? Or had they addressed them to the wrong person? They did not feel that they had attended a church service. It had seemed amateurish in comparison to services they had attended in orthodox churches. There was no message or spiritual guidance contained in the talk, as there would have been in a sermon. It was merely a series of anecdotes strung together. The prayers were long, repetitive and without meaning. It was not surprising that the congregation was sparse compared to the church further up the road.

On the plus side, they both felt that the younger medium appeared to give true messages, although they could not judge how accurate he had been, because he did not speak to either of them. So where did they go next? They did not fancy another visit to a Spiritualist church. They had hoped it would have provided the answers to their questions, but it had repelled them. They could not see themselves ever being part of it. Perhaps they were unfortunate in encountering such a poor ambassador on their first visit. Or had they not been fair to the man? There was a chance that they had not seen him at his best. After all, everyone can have an off night. Perhaps, by expecting immediate and specific answers to their questions, they had not given him a chance to get through to them. There was also the possibility that it was they who were at fault: they did not listen because he did not tell them what they wanted to hear.

Whatever the reason, the image of that cold, cheerless room stayed with them for a very long time. There did not seem to be any happiness or brightness in that church. It had not lit a spark in them, answered their questions or created a desire to return to its sombre atmosphere.

Should they try another Spiritualist church? Would they be wasting their time? It would not cost much. Fifty pence in the collection and the cost of a few raffle tickets was a cheap night out by anyone's standards. Yet did they want to repeat the experience, and risk further disillusionment? They thought long and hard, and spent hours discussing the 'pros' and 'cons' of their venture into Spiritualism, before making their decision.

Spiritualism was definitely not for them.

# Chapter Four

The weeks following their visit to the church were hectic. The school holidays had begun and it was the riding school's busiest time of the year. They were fully booked every day except Monday, which was the horses' day off. The stable yard was full from dawn to dusk with excited, chattering children and their proud parents. Amy had her hands full talking to parents and making sure that neither the children nor the ponies got up to any mischief.

In an effort to get back to full time employment following his illness, Geoff had begun to manufacture show jumps. It was a purely physical job which he could do without stress or having to leave the property. He was not yet allowed to drive, so working at home seemed to be the ideal solution.

As if Amy had not enough to do, she was given the job of chief painter. Most of her 'spare' time was spent in splashing poles with a variety of bright colours, followed by evenings in the bath scrubbing the paint off. Tim, Amy's shadow, had a habit of leaning against walls and anything upright, like the show jump wings. As a result he sported a rainbow coloured coat.

There was not enough time in the day, and certainly no time for Amy to think about explanations for her new found psychic ability. She had not abandoned her search, merely put it to one side until she could devote some time to it. Long summer nights did not lend themselves to matters of the paranormal. There were much more pressing jobs to be done.

It was about this time that she began to hear loud cracking noises coming from the wooden headboard directly above her head. She did not connect these noises with 'rappings', or 'knockings', which are associated with spirit communication, as they were completely different from the knocks she had heard at the end of the séance. She thought it might be that the headboard was shrinking as the room cooled, but never asked Geoff's opinion. Somehow, she felt he might not take her seriously.

Little did she know that she was experiencing the same type of phenomenon as that which led to the birth of Modern Spiritualism. In March 1848, the Fox family were plagued by loud knocking in their home in Hydesville, New York. Two of the children experimented and found that by establishing a code they could ask questions and receive answers. This ultimately led to the phenomenon being publicly demonstrated, and the rest is history.

Amy knew nothing of this and it never entered her head to attempt to reply to the knocks, as she did not associate them with the knocks she had heard during the séance. Although they were very loud, the noises never woke Geoff up. Even if they had, it would have been highly unlikely that Amy would have been able to persuade him to join her in talking to the headboard.

Ivan was creeping back into her thoughts at night and was never far away from them during the day. Where was he? Was he well? Was he dead? Why could she not get him out of her mind? She had no illusions of rekindling their affair. They had both lived their own lives, which had not included each other. She did not believe that she could go back and expect their relationship to be as it was. She was a completely different person: her character had been formed through her experiences of life, none of which had included him. Her daughters were very precious to her and she was very happy with the man she had.

Now that he was in her thoughts, she felt that she would like to know how the world had treated him and whether or not he was alive. She had exhausted all available channels of investigation and had neither the inclination nor the funds to employ someone to find him. Then one night she woke up with the answer. She found herself sitting bolt upright in bed saying out loud, "Of course! He's in Australia!"

Then things began to make sense. While they had walked out together, Ivan had attempted to teach her about astronomy. He had pointed out various constellations and told her their names. She could never tell them apart, but nodded and told him how clever he was, which was what young ladies did in 1958.

For some time, whenever Ivan came to mind, she had closed her eyes in an effort to visualise him. His face never appeared. All she could see was a constellation of stars. She did not recognise the constellation until she saw it during the final credits of an Australian soap. It was the Southern Cross, only visible from the southern hemisphere. It was possible that he had emigrated to Australia, which would explain why she could find no trace of him. After being obsessed with finding him, she now found that she did not really care. He remained in the back of her mind as a distant memory, but the urgency to find him had disappeared.

Then she had another dream. It was short: over in a moment, but it was very clear. In it she was looking down at a man, who was seated, facing her. He was holding a small golden horseshoe in his hand, which he offered to her. She did not recognise the man and forgot about the dream until she went into the stable yard the next morning.

The yard was full of riders waiting for their mounts. She called out their names, allocating a pony to each of them then she noticed a discarded horseshoe on the ground. She asked her stable lad, who was waiting to escort the ride, if he knew which pony had cast a shoe. He replied that he had checked them all and their shoes were all tight. Then she found that the shoe was from a pony that was not working that day.

The shoe brought the dream flooding back. As the riders filed down the drive for the first ride of the day, Carolyn, one of Amy's friends, arrived and parked her car behind the stables. Amy held the shoe up.

*"That's broken my dream,"* she said.

*"Oh, have you had another one?"* Carolyn's eyes lit up. She loved hearing about the now famous dreams. *"Tell me about it."*

*"Put the kettle on."* said Amy. *"I'll take a coffee out for Geoff then we'll be able to talk in peace."*

Geoff was in the workshop. She had not told him about her paranormal experiences, so she did not want him interrupting them while they discussed the dream.

Once they were settled, Amy told Carolyn what she had seen in her dream. She explained that, although the man in the dream was a stranger, she had the feeling that the horseshoe was a gift from her father.

*"It might be his way of wishing you good luck with the show jumps,"* suggested Carolyn. *"It's about time you had some. You've had enough trouble over the past few years to last a lifetime."*

This was true, for in the space of six years, Geoff had nearly died when he was operated on for a brain tumour; their shop had burned down; one of their staff had stolen thousands of pounds from their business; Amy was in litigation with a large company who had polluted her grazing and the miners' strike had just finished.

Many of the locals relied on the mines, either directly or indirectly, for their living, so the whole economy of the area was affected by the strike. Amy's business had also suffered. The locals had little money for essentials, much less riding lessons.

Carolyn's husband was a miner, and she worked in the coal board offices. During the strike she had helped in the school. She was not paid, but worked with the horses because she loved them and because it occupied her time. She was very glad when the strike ended and they could both return to work.

By this time, so many of Amy's dreams had proved to be true that they both took the horseshoe as a sign that good luck was on its way. There was no time to discuss it further, for the ride was on its way back and Amy had to be ready to supervise the next group of riders who were already waiting in the yard.

The dream was soon forgotten in the bustle of Sunday's work.

On Monday, the horses' day off, she painted poles: they had a large order to get ready by the weekend. Part of this order was for jump cups, the adjustable metal fixtures which were pinned onto the wings to support the poles. Amy had approached various blacksmiths the previous week, leaving a template with each of them and asking for a quote for a large quantity of jump cups. As the family's finances were restricted, it was important that she should obtain the keenest price possible in order to compete with other manufacturers.

The last of the tenders arrived in the post on Tuesday morning and Amy accepted the lowest quote. She had to go to the bank that morning and would be passing one of the blacksmiths, so she decided to call in and collect her template. The forge was a family concern which employed a number of men and was situated on a main road. The owner came out to talk to her when he heard her asking for the template. When she told him that she had accepted a lower quote, he became annoyed and asked if she was having the job done 'on the side' by a pit blacksmith. She retorted that she most certainly was not, as she disagreed with 'moonlighting'.

He calmed down and began to talk about the general state of business. When she told him that she also bred horses, and was interested in National Hunt racing, his attitude changed and he became very friendly.

*"I used to be a registered farrier,"* he said. *"Come upstairs into the office. I'll show you pictures of some of the horses I used to shoe."*

He was surprised and delighted when she recognised the horses whose photographs decorated his office walls and knew a little of their racing history. She explained her knowledge by saying that the jockey in the pictures was the son of the man who owned the livery yard where she had worked when she left school. They talked for some time, about horses and 'the good old days'. He was pleased to find someone who shared his interest.

He went to the other side of the desk, sat down, then reached into the top right hand drawer. She caught her breath when he handed up to her a small, shiny, brass plated horseshoe. It glittered like gold and she could hardly believe her eyes. Then she recognised him as the man she had seen in her dream. It had happened just as she had dreamed! Turning the shoe in her hands, she asked if he was giving it to her. He said he was and found some horseshoe nails to hang it up.

She told him about the dream. He smiled and said she was more than welcome to the shoe and he hoped it would bring her good luck. He explained that it was a replica brass plated racing plate, scaled down and used as the symbol of a farrier. She thanked him once more then left.

She sat for some time in her rusty old van, collecting her thoughts and trying to rationalise what had happened. Placing the horseshoe on the dashboard, she traced its outline with her finger. She could neither see nor feel her father, but thought that he must surely be there. She removed her shopping from the passenger seat, as if making room for him to sit down. This might appear silly, but it seemed to her that it was the right thing to do. Besides, who was to know? There was nobody in the van other than herself and her dad.

She believed that he had arranged for her to receive the horseshoe as an unsolicited gift from a complete stranger. It was a tangible piece of evidence that she could hold in her hand whenever she felt lonely. Added to her other experiences, she was now convinced that there must be life after death. She realised then that she had never been alone, just unaware of her spirit companions. It was a wonderful feeling to know that somebody cared. She was loved. She would never walk alone again.

As she waited for the traffic to clear, looking one way then the other, her eyes were drawn to the faded notice board in the garden of the tiny chapel next to the forge. She could only just make out what it said. It was a Spiritualist church! Intrigued, she reversed the van back into the car park and inspected the notice more closely. The paint was peeling, but she was able to make out that there was an open circle once a week. This really was too much of a coincidence. Not only had her father given her the horseshoe, she felt that he had directed her to this church. She drove off, determined to come back, with or without a companion.

Some might consider that she had jumped to conclusions and had twisted the meaning to suit her purpose. However, there was no disputing the fact that she had foreseen the blacksmith's gift, because she had shared the dream with Carolyn two days before she met the man. She had passed the little chapel hundreds of times without giving it a second glance and had never known that it was a Spiritualist church. The series of events that led her to the church made her feel that her father had directed her there. Without the dream she would never have considered entering a Spiritualist church again.

Carolyn called the following evening and Amy told her what had happened at the forge. She related the story exactly as it had happened, producing the horseshoe from behind her back with an elaborate, theatrical flourish.

*"My goodness! I've gone all goose pimply!"* cried Carolyn, holding out her arms to show the goose bumps.

Needless to say, she was also keen to go to the church. She told her friends at work, so it was a large group, including Pauline, which descended on the little Spiritualist church. From the minute she entered the church Amy felt that she was supposed to be there. Their group tried to sit at the back, but were encouraged by the chairman to sit within the circle. It was a cosy little church and she was soon at her ease. The chairs were placed in a large circle at the front of the church and they filled up rapidly as the time for the service to start drew near.

The chairman welcomed everyone and explained how the service would be conducted. He also explained how to answer a medium should one come to you. Amy felt happier in this circle. Nobody was allowed to monopolise the floor and all the mediums were at different stages of development. One man was quick, to the point and full of humour, while others took longer to get their messages across. Amy got a message that night, but it was from a novice medium and although it did contain a small scrap of evidence, it consisted mainly of names, which many others could have understood, without supporting information which would have identified the communicating spirit. It was also a little drawn out. Nevertheless, she decided that this was the place where she could learn about what was happening to her. Carolyn also got a message concerning her grandmother and was keen to return.

What made the two churches so different? Why had they been repelled by one, yet attracted to the other? I do not suppose that one church was any better than the other, but a lot does depend on what is going on within the church at the time. Churches are what their members make them. Because of this they, too can have bad days. At this point in her development Amy needed a church in which she felt comfortable, where her new psychic awareness could flourish and grow. This church seemed to fill those needs.

During the next few months she steeped herself in Spiritualism. She never missed a service. Constantly looking for answers, she asked many questions, some of which were answered to her satisfaction, while others were not. One or two of the answers made her think, leading to more questions. Some of the church regulars were only too pleased to give her the benefit of their knowledge, while others were not. Although the latter were happy to demonstrate their own psychic ability, they were jealous of what little knowledge they had and did not appear to be willing to pass it on. Luckily, these were in the minority, but Amy felt that their actions belied their preaching.

There was so much that she needed to know. She had found the place she had been looking for and could see no reason to waste any more time. The more she learned, the more she wanted to learn. She was impatient, expecting an instant answer to everything. Soon she was being told to slow down, to allow the answers to come to her. Much later, she realised that she must have appeared to be a nuisance, because she asked for advice, then, if it was different to what she felt it should be, ignored it.

However, she was a reasonably intelligent, thinking person and found it hard to accept anything that she considered illogical or wrong.

Spiritualists are no different from any other group of people and they come in all shapes and sizes. They may try to live a more spiritual existence, but they are human, so are subject to the failings associated with the physical body. They all seemed to have their own ideas regarding Spiritualism, so it was no wonder that Amy became confused as she listened to conflicting versions of the same subject.

There were a lot of old wives' tales, also: 'do's' and 'don'ts', which did not make sense to her. Some of it even insulted her intelligence, but she was too polite to say so. She worked on the principle that this was their church; their religion: as a newcomer she should adopt a watching attitude until she knew what she was talking about. She learned to accept what she felt was right for her and to put to one side things she thought were wrong. She also found that, as her knowledge grew, she could understand some of the things she had previously put to one side.

It was about this time that she began to see faces when she closed her eyes at night. It was as if she had a television set in her mind, with faces flashing on the screen at regular intervals. She often lay in bed for an hour or more, watching them as they flashed before her closed eyes. She did not recognise any of them, but they kept coming. Eventually she became annoyed at this procession of strange faces that paraded before her each night. She thought, which she felt was the way to communicate with the spirits,

*"Why do you bring me these strange faces every night? Can't you show me someone that I would recognise?"*

Instantly the faces stopped coming and the 'television screen' went blank. Then a man's face began to build up and she recognised him immediately as her grandfather, who had died in 1945. It was then that she realised that the communications she received could be controlled: she was a transmitter as well as a receiver.

She also began to see pictures in her mind as she sat, with her eyes closed, during the meditation in the open circle. Pauline also experienced this, but none of the others who had come with them originally did. One by one they lost interest and stopped coming to the church. More often than not, Amy went to the church on her own, as there were times when Pauline was on night shift. Sometimes, as mediums gave one of the other sitters a message, Amy found that they were describing thoughts and pictures she had in her mind. She did not realise that she was 'linking in' to the same vibrations as the medium. They were both experiencing the same thoughts, the difference being that the mediums were in control and able to turn themselves on and off like a tap. They could also recognise when what they received was symbolic and so translate whatever they saw into a message for one of the sitters.

As she watched the mediums work, Amy sometimes felt drawn to one of the sitters. As she watched them she found herself making stories up about them in her mind. When she closed her eyes she would see vivid pictures which illustrated the thoughts. Then one night she felt as if someone was pushing her from behind. She was being urged to get to her feet.

The first time that she stood up in the open circle surprised her as much as it did anyone else. She had felt drawn to a middle aged woman. As she watched the woman she saw pictures of a man, his face dirty, as if he had been down the mines. His clothes were in shreds: they hung around him in tatters, and his toes poked out of his gaping boots. He looked as if he had gone to a fancy dress party as a tramp but had gone over the top with his costume. Then Amy heard a name in her mind, and saw a picture of an umbrella.

As soon as the medium who was giving a message sat down, Amy got to her feet. She was aware that the chairman was surprised and that more than one pair of eyes that watched her were critical.

She had thought that she would be self conscious, but was too busy concentrating on getting the message right to bother about being watched. As she spoke to the woman, her self consciousness disappeared. She told the woman what she had seen, told her the name, and that she had seen an umbrella. Amy did not know who was the most surprised when the message was accepted: the woman, or herself.

The woman spoke to Amy after the service, and explained that the man in rags had been her father. He had identified himself by illustrating a memory of an event which had happened during the blitz in London. He had returned home one day with his clothes in tatters and his toes sticking out of his boots. When she saw him she had laughed, telling him that he looked like a tramp. He became annoyed when she laughed and explained that he had survived a blast that had killed his best friend. The woman told Amy that she had given her evidence that she had waited years to hear. Amy could not have known anything about this woman's father, as this was the first time they had spoken. This was an unusual memory which dated back forty five years. Nobody knew it about other than the woman and her father. The woman also accepted the name, which she had to think about before remembering, and she said that her father had given her an umbrella that he had won in a raffle.

'Gobsmacked' is the only word that could come near to describing the way Amy felt after the woman spoke to her. Then she realised that she was not making stories up about the people she watched. She was not imagining things. She was mediumistic.

# Chapter Five

By now Geoff knew that Amy was attending a Spiritualist church, or 'spooky chapel', as he preferred to call it. He did not say much, but treated it as her latest whim and was prepared to indulge her, as usual. He felt that it would pass and she would lose interest. At least it did not cost very much and when she went to church there was no danger that she would come home with yet another horse. However, he did complain when she began attending extra services, so she restricted her visits to the church to two a week.

Her friends and relatives reacted in different ways, varying from resigned acceptance, in Geoff's case, to a shaking of heads and warnings not to 'dabble with that sort of thing'. Amy took no notice. Her burning desire to learn more about Spiritualism made her deaf to criticism. Things had happened: she had taken the first steps: she would not be satisfied until she knew everything there was to know. She had no idea of the enormity of task she had set herself. As she finished one chapter of discovery, there was always another to tempt her. Even getting to the end of a book did not qualify her to say she knew it all: there would always be a sequel.

She could not get enough of Spiritualism and attended church as often as she could, sometimes with Pauline. Other times she went alone. She occasionally received a message from one of the mediums, but never one concerning Ivan. Perhaps he was not dead after all, but alive and well and living 'down under'. Finding Ivan did not matter any more. He was not the reason she went to church, but she began to feel that perhaps he had been the carrot to tempt her into Spiritualism.

She attended the Sunday divine service at the church as well as the open circle, but was often disappointed with the content. She had expected that every medium who stood on the platform of a Spiritualist church would be a good public speaker. This was not the case. Sometimes it was very difficult to hear them at all. Even at that early stage, when she knew little about Spiritualism, she could see that she was not going to learn much from some of the 'philosophies' delivered from the platform of her church.

Her thirst for knowledge could not be slaked at such services, where the 'philosophy' often consisted of a poetry reading or an account of a personal experience. Very few mediums spoke of the philosophy of Spiritualism, which was what she wanted to know about. Perhaps she was expecting too much, but I hardly think so. She had always aspired to do things to a high standard. If she could not reach that standard in any particular activity, she gave it up and concentrated on things she could do well. So it is no wonder that she failed to see why some mediums did such a poor job yet continued to accept bookings. What puzzled her even more was that the church officials continued to book them.

There is always a difference in workmanship in every sphere and mediumship is no exception. However, not all the church services were bad, not by any means. Some were good, some very good, while one or two actually inspired her.

As with most truthful and honest people, it was not long before Amy's mouth got her into trouble in the church. She made the mistake of giving her opinion of a service when it was asked for. The look of superiority and disgust that she received from the woman who had asked for her opinion startled her. She was told that she should not criticize speakers when she did not know what she was talking about, or unless she could do a better job herself.

Amy would normally have entered into a debate with this woman, but she backed down in deference to the fact that the woman had been a Spiritualist for many years and should have known what she was talking about. However, she had heard the same woman criticize mediums, but what she had said had been of a personal nature and not confined to platform presentation. There ends the first lesson.

She had as little to do with that woman as was possible in such a small church. Whatever she said to the woman, or within her earshot, was twisted out of all recognition and Amy heard herself being misquoted by her on many occasions. However, there were many very pleasant people in the church, so Amy concentrated on them and their more positive attitude.

It was not long before Amy realised that the church was not a magic cottage where all would be revealed to her. If she really wanted to learn she would have to work hard for every scrap of knowledge she gained.

Within Spiritualism, as in any organisation, the individual branches, in this case the churches, display different standards. They are run by people and people are all different. As in other organisation, there is often upheaval and mini power struggles as members engage in the politics of administration. On rare occasions the membership is divided into those who matter and those who don't. Those who matter have a say in what happens in the church and feel it is their right to change things, whereas those who don't matter are expected to turn up to services, put their money in the collection plate and keep their opinions to themselves.

Amy's wish to know more about Spiritualism made her bite her tongue on many occasions and turn up the next night like a good little girl, hoping that this would be the night she would learn something new. She did not realise that she accumulated knowledge every time she walked through the doors of the church. Even those mediums whose services were poor had something to teach her. They showed her how not to do it. Whenever she had to sit through one of these poor services she reasoned that it was not Spiritualism at fault, it was the medium. What made it all worthwhile was when a medium stood on the rostrum and gave an inspiring philosophy followed by a convincing demonstration of clairvoyance. On those occasions she left the church with a spring in her step, a warm glow inside her, with new thoughts and ideas planted like seeds in her mind.

One medium really did light a spark within her. He was a middle aged, no nonsense sort of a man and his talk reflected the knowledge that he had of his religion. This was a man who could reach out and touch your very soul with his philosophy and his demonstration of mediumship was even better.

Amy found that she was sitting up a little straighter, longing for him to come to her with a message. She had no doubt that this man really could communicate with the spirit world, for the information he gave was specific and accurate. With one eye on the clock she began to panic. The chairperson would be calling the medium to time soon, and he had not even looked her way. Then she felt as if someone had placed a hand on her shoulder and whispered into her ear

*"Relax. The last message is for you."*

She relaxed and watched the medium. Then she blinked hard and rubbed her eyes, for she could no longer see him. Superimposed over him was the figure of a bishop. She stared and blinked again, but the bishop remained. He finished a message and turned to look at her.

*"May I speak with you?"* he asked and when she replied *'yes'*, he proceeded to relay messages from her grandmother and grandfather, naming them both and giving their relationship to each other and to her.

This was what a Spiritualist medium was! Her heart sang as she drove home. After seeing this man and listening to what he had to say, she knew that she was not alone and she knew where she wanted to be. He really had ignited a spark within her, giving her a standard to aim for and proving to her that his religion was what she wanted for herself.

There is always a danger that, when you find something new and wonderful like Spiritualism, you will turn into a bore. Amy was no exception. There is nothing more off putting than a zealous convert who embarks on a mission to steer others onto the 'right path'.

She tried to convince everyone she knew, regardless of their religion, that Spiritualism would change their lives as it had hers. She did not make many converts, but some people began to avoid engaging her in conversation.

I suppose that some of them thought that Amy had finally flipped. At that point in her development she could not see that what she had discovered, no matter how wonderful it was to her personally, did not have the same impact on others. You cannot really blame them for being sceptical. Her story did sound strange and it got no better as she repeated it.

Now she had discovered that she was mediumistic, where did she go next? Working on the platform of a Spiritualist church did not appeal to her at all. Many mediums did not appear at ease as they stood on the platform and it seemed such a serious business: not something Amy wanted to subject herself to. They often paced the rostrum, faces deadly serious as they reached for evidence of survival to pass on to the congregation. Some of them played with the lectern or screwed up their handkerchiefs, nervous gestures which gave the impression that they were not happy in their work.

At this point the reader may wonder why Amy continued to go to the church if she felt that there was so much wrong with it. She did not consciously search for faults, but she was new enough to Spiritualism to be able to look at it with the eye of an outsider. Her vision was not influenced by rose coloured glasses and she was not the type of person who had blind faith. She was a paying customer and expected certain things from a service. Above all, things had to make sense.

Watching mediums work educated Amy in the 'do's' and 'don'ts' of mediumship. It is a great responsibility to stand on the platform and have the congregation's undivided attention as they listen to your philosophy and accepting (or not) your evidence of survival. The words a medium speaks from the rostrum may be the sparks that ignite a desire to learn more, or the wet blanket that douses the flame lit by others. Amy never forgot how she was repelled on her first visit to a Spiritualist church. First impressions are sometimes last impressions. Others having a similar experience may decide, as Amy and Pauline originally did, that Spiritualism was not right for them.

Amy knew that those who had given her this impression had been well meaning and were probably hard workers in the church. Yet being a hard worker, or holding a key position in the church does not necessarily make one a good ambassador. She had been guided back to Spiritualism, but that does not happen with everyone.

She did not accept Spiritualism without spending hours weighing the evidence. She often discussed the content of services with Pauline, going over all that was said and done until they reached an opinion on its merit. Although Pauline did not attend the church as regularly as Amy, she was just as keen. One night, after the open circle, Pauline was chatting with Sam, one of the more experienced mediums. During the conversation she mentioned the Horse of the Year Show room. Sam felt that the old man probably did not realise that he had passed over and should be helped on his way. He offered to come to the house and see if he could persuade the old man's spirit to move on. Amy was not sure that he would be able to do this, but he seemed confident that he could, so she agreed. He also booked a beach ride, saying he would combine business with pleasure.

Amy decided that it would be prudent for Sam to come when the riding school was normally closed. However, the news that a medium was coming to the house to take the old man away ensured that there were plenty of witnesses. Pauline, Liz, (another friend of Amy's,) Carolyn and Teresa were all keen to be there.

Pauline and Sam went out for a ride then came back for coffee. As they sat around the morning room table, Sam began to 'tune in', to see what he could pick up about the old man. He mentioned golf balls, which Amy knew applied to one of the previous occupants of the houses, who had been a keen golfer. Then he said he was ready to go upstairs.

Sam allowed Amy to come to the top of the stairs, but he went into the bedroom alone and closed the door behind him. The others stood on the stairs and strained their ears to hear what Sam was saying to the old man. Amy ventured past the bedroom door towards the bathroom, while the others took her place and clustered together at the top of the stairs. They could hear a conversation going on in the Horse of the year Show room. Sam seemed to be reasoning with the old man. Then he raised his voice. Suddenly, Amy felt a rush of icy air. Startled, she cried out. Sam rushed out of the bedroom, and looked around as if he was searching for someone.

*"Where does that door lead to?"* he asked, pointing over Amy's shoulder.

*"The bathroom,"* she replied.

*"He's gone in there."* Sam said, squeezing past Amy.

He went into the bathroom and resumed his conversation with the old man, who appeared to be standing in the bath. Amy could not see him, but she had no doubt that Sam could.

*"Why is he standing in the bath?"* asked Sam.

*"We changed the bathroom around when we moved in."* replied Amy. There was a space where the bath is now."

Gradually, Sam persuaded the old man to return to the bedroom. By this time Amy and the others were all wondering what would happen next. Then they heard another voice, with a local dialect, arguing with Sam. At times they could hear both voices at once. Clearly, the old man needed some persuasion to leave 'his' room. After a lot of negotiating, Sam came out.

*"He's accepted that he doesn't belong here any more,"* he said, *"He has agreed to leave, but for some reason, he's not sure about coming downstairs. Have you changed the staircase?"*

Amy confirmed that they had moved the staircase and changed the direction of the stairs. Instead of being in a passage that divided two small rooms, the stairs were now against the wall of one large room.

*"I want you all to go downstairs,"* said Sam. *"I'm going to take the old man inside my body to get him down the stairs. Nobody*

*should talk, or get in my way. Amy, make sure all the doors are open so I can go straight out."*

He disappeared into the bedroom and they all went downstairs, talking in whispers. They had all individually heard what appeared to be the old man's voice, but were not sure if the others had heard him, too. When Sam reappeared they did not recognise him. His face had changed shape, and his posture had altered as he walked hesitantly down the stairs. Slowly, looking about him with vacant eyes, he made his way through the living room, into the morning room, then into the kitchen. Amy went in front of him, making sure his way was clear. She held the back door open, and he walked onto the lawn then fell on his knees.

They did not know what to do. Should they ask him if he needed help? Should they try to get him onto his feet? He had instructed them not to touch him, so they thought it best to leave him where he was. Nobody had either the experience or knowledge to help him, although Pauline would have done something if she had thought he was in any physical danger.

*"Come on,"* said Amy, closing the back door, *"I reckon that he knows what he's doing. Carolyn, make some coffee. I'm sure he'll need a drink."*

Later, over coffee, Sam was subdued. Taking the old man away appeared to have drained his energy. He explained that the old man had told him he had been looking through some junk in the room when he had a heart attack. He lay for a while, hoping that a woman, whom he referred to as Mary, would come back from shopping. When she did find him, he had died. His spirit had not realised that he was dead and was still waiting for Mary to come home to help him.

When Sam announced that he was going home, Amy asked him how much she owed him, but he refused to accept any money. He then attempted to pay for his ride, but Amy felt justified in saying that it was 'on the house'. Sam was not himself for many months after this, and later admitted that he should have never attempted to remove the old man on his own.

After he left, and many times since, the friends discussed what had happened. They checked their individual experiences with each other, and found that they were all the same. Pauline had noticed Amy jump as the old man rushed past her and they had all heard two different voices coming from the room. Weeks passed and there was no sign of the old man (not even on the lawn!), so they felt that Sam really had taken their ghost away. They had witnessed an exorcism!

It had been quite tame, not nearly as dramatic as they had expected. Of course, they had not expected Sam to fall on the floor, spurting green vomit and talking in tongues, as they do in films. Or had they?

Neither Amy nor Pauline had taken up the offer to become members of the church. Attending a Spiritualist church was one thing. Becoming members meant committing themselves to the religion and they did not think they knew enough about it to make this commitment. However, in early November, the church president persuaded them to become associate members of the church. This would enable them to go to the church Christmas party. Not the best of reasons to join any organisation, but they did.

Two weeks later, Pauline dropped a bombshell. She had previously applied for a job in Saudi Arabia and had received news that she had been accepted. At first she thought she was going away in January, then she was asked to travel two days before Christmas. There was so much to do in such a short time. Pauline is an inveterate hoarder, who never discards anything that may one day come in useful. She rented a double lock up garage and filled it with possessions that she felt she had to hold on to. Geoff helped her to move and pack her belongings, but there was still a large quantity left. This was stored in the Horses of the Year Show room.

Before Amy had time to get used to the idea that Pauline was leaving, her friend was gone. Now she was on her own. This did not stop her from attending the church, but she still felt that she was on the outside looking in. She needed more than the displays of mediumship at the open circles and Sunday services. She was no longer looking for evidence that man survived physical death, for she had her horseshoe, which was proof enough for her. There had to be something more than just phenomena.

She had not attended a church regularly since her schooldays until now. Christianity had lost its appeal. She had tried it, studied it and turned her back on it. She had no problem with the Old Testament and the history of the Hebrews, but felt that the New Testament seemed one sided and difficult to believe. She had no beliefs, merely disbeliefs. Now she was becoming aware that there was something lacking in her life.

Everyone has to believe in something. Perhaps Amy was coming to the age when people tend to adopt a more spiritual way of life. If you look at the congregations of churches of all denominations, middle aged and elderly people are usually in the majority. Does this mean that, when a person reaches a certain age he adopts religion as an insurance policy? Was Amy embracing Spiritualism because she was approaching this age and needed to believe that physical death was not the end of her life?

This may have been a contributory factor, but it would not explain why she suddenly began to have psychic experiences. When she gave messages to people in the open circle she got very few negative responses. If those people were being truthful, she had to be getting this information from somewhere. It could not all originate in her head.

She wrestled with this problem, trying to understand how and why she had made her way to the church. She reasoned that, if the messages were really from people who had 'passed over', then there must be a spirit world. What form this spirit world took was a mystery to her, but she felt that there had to be some place where they all existed. If there was a spirit world, was it then not possible there was also a supreme being?

This made sense to her. After years of ignorance she was beginning to see the light. She had found her pathway to God.

# Chapter Six

The last words of the previous chapter may have confused the reader, for many people do not recognise Spiritualism as a religion. How could Amy have found her pathway to God through it? Anyone with an orthodox religious upbringing may find it difficult to believe that she had, for isn't Spiritualism against all they have been taught? It is only a little more than three hundred years since witches were burned at the stake in Britain by people who practiced orthodox religions. Amy considered herself lucky to have been born in a more enlightened age, where 'different' people, like her, are tolerated.

There was not an education programme in the church at that time. Newcomers were expected to pick up things as best they could. There was a library of sorts, but the books in it were either written in outdated language or were very basic. They were also nearly all in very poor condition. All Amy had access to, as she prepared to adopt this new religion, were the Seven Principles of Spiritualism, which every Spiritualist is expected to accept. She picked up scraps of information, like crumbs from a table, by listening and watching church members who had experience, and theoretically, knowledge of their religion. However, it was not long before she reached a point where she realised that their knowledge was limited, but they themselves had not attempted to look any further. This was not enough for her.

After a while she did discovered, and attended, the healing services. Like many horsewomen, she had lower back pain and found that Spiritualist healing relieved this. Worn vertebrae in her lower spine had troubled her for many years. Now and then one of her discs would 'slip'. When this happened she was bedridden for up to a fortnight. Painkillers did not help, so she had to lie as flat and still as possible until she was well enough to visit the osteopath.

After a few visits to the healing service, her back was much better and the discs stayed in their place. She has not had a 'slipped' disc for more than eighteen years.

Pain, especially the spasms of back pain, can be a powerful weapon in changing people's minds. One of Amy and Geoff's friends, Stuart, who had sold Bobby to them, also suffered with his back. He built dry stone walls for a living and found that he was having more and more time off work due to his back. One night Geoff laughingly suggested that Stuart should go to the 'spooky chapel'.

*"They cured Amy's back. Maybe they can do the same for you,"* he said.

Stuart was going home the following day, so would not be able to attend the healing service at the church. Amy telephoned the church president and asked if Stuart would be able to have healing after the open circle that night. The president said that he would arrange this.

Geoff thought it was a great joke when Stuart accompanied Amy to the open circle and even funnier when he came back without experiencing any relief from his healing session. Stuart was very sheepish. He had gone to the church as a last resort. As other treatments had failed, he had nothing to lose except, possibly, his dignity. As he went to bed that night, with Geoff's good natured teasing ringing in his ears, he regretted going to the church.

When Amy woke the next morning everyone was downstairs. As she dressed she heard peals of laughter coming from the morning room. When she investigated she found that Susan had cooked breakfast, and the three of them were sharing a joke.

*"What's so funny?"* asked Amy, sitting at the table.

Geoff was wiping his eyes, and attempted to say something, but all he could manage was, *"Stuart got out of bed."*

*"What he's trying to say is that I got out of bed this morning and my back was grand. I could put my socks on without any effort or pain, so I went for a walk along the cliffs. I haven't done anything like that for years."*

*"That's good. The healing must have worked, after all. But what's so funny about that?"* Amy asked.

*"Well, all I said was I wasn't sure whether or not I was dreaming, that I was expecting to wake up any minute and struggle downstairs to find you lot laughing at me for going to the spooky chapel."*

Stuart's back was not miraculously cured. The damage done to it over a period of years cannot be mended, but the healing could have given him relief from the pain. Now it was up to him to look after himself and respect the fact that he had a damaged spine. Healing, like conventional medicine, is wasted if the condition is aggravated by continual abuse of the injury. When Stuart returned home he felt so much better that he went back to work. As soon as he lifted a heavy load in the wrong manner he hurt his back again. Whenever he visited them after that, he went with Amy to the church for more healing.

Amy felt she was living two lives. Her husband and friends were not interested in the Spiritualist church. With the exception of Pauline, all of her friends had lost interest when the prognostic dreams ceased. Spiritualist phenomena fascinated them, but they shied away from it as a religion. As a result, Amy went from being 'interesting' to 'weird'. Those who had once hung on her every word now changed the subject when she began to talk about the church. Pauline was the only one who remained constant in her interest, but she could hardly pop on a plane from Saudi to accompany Amy to the open circle.

Whenever she saw couples, or groups of friends attending the church together, Amy felt envious. Her relationship with Geoff allowed each of them to be their own person, with their own beliefs and disbeliefs. They did not agree on many subjects, but neither had attempted to impose their will or belief on the other. Spiritualism was something that Amy felt she could not discuss with Geoff, because he refused to enter into serious discussion on a subject that he considered to be frivolous. Amy always had the feeling that he was waiting for her to tire of Spiritualism, or to have her eyes opened so that she could see it for what he thought it was.

At this moment in time there was no chance of that. The church had become her haven. It was completely different from her daily life and was a refuge when things got on top of her. Yet a comfortable church with a pleasant congregation never seemed enough for her. What was she seeking? To tell the truth, I do not think she knew the answer herself.

As she worked in the open circle, Amy realised that she did not have complete control of her gift. She occasionally went to the wrong person with a message and would waste time until someone claimed the message as theirs. Amy found this hard, for everything she had ever learned before had come so easily to her. If she was not good at any subject or activity she usually gave it up. Spiritualism was different. She knew that the only way to improve was to use the gift she had been given, for practice makes perfect. As long as she learned from her mistakes, she would improve.

An open circle is designed for novice mediums. It gives them the opportunity to sit in a circle of like minded people and gain experience within a positive atmosphere. She struggled on, trying to master her budding mediumship and improve it to a standard that she felt was acceptable.

To doubt is a human failing. If it cannot be seen, or touched, it has to be proven that it exists. Amy had doubts, too. She turned any evidence she received over in her mind, examining it thoroughly before accepting it as true. It went further than the giving and receiving of messages. She saw Spiritualism as a way of life, not just a means of communicating with departed spirits.

The congregations in the church included people from all walks of life. As in other religions, there were a large number of elderly women, but they by no means made up the whole membership. There were younger people, too: nurses, teachers, factory workers, housewives, people of all shapes and sizes. They all had credibility and Amy could relate to them. Many of them had independently experienced similar psychic phenomena to Amy and she reasoned that they could not all be suffering from some type of mass hallucination. Listening to their stories, she realised how common psychic phenomena is and how many different forms it takes. However, she was not prepared for what happened next.

One night she set off for church, disregarding Geoff's warning that she should stay at home. There was a storm raging, with gale force winds and the only vehicle available to her was a transit van. They had just purchased it and Amy had never driven a transit before, so Geoff was naturally concerned that she insisted on going to church. Amy was confident that she could manage and was determined not to miss the open circle, so she set off.

The van was empty, which made it more susceptible to the strong winds. It was buffeted by these winds as she drove slowly along the almost deserted road. She had to cross two bridges, where the wind almost tore the steering wheel from her grasp. She was grateful that it was a dual carriageway and there was little chance of hitting a vehicle coming the other way, but when she reached the most exposed parts of the road, her heart was in her mouth as she edged the van forwards at fifteen miles an hour. Her determination to get to church helped to subdue her fears as the van rocked from side to side. It took all her strength to keep it on the right side of the road, which was mercifully free from traffic. Only the foolhardy and desperate had braved the storm that night and she was not sure which category she was in. Perhaps she was a little of both.

By the time she reached the church, she was a few minutes late and she heard the congregation singing the opening hymn as she approached the heavy outer door. To her amazement, the door would not open. It was locked. She tried the handle and pushed against the door, but it remained tightly closed. She could have knocked, but did not want to disturb the service. She could not understand why anyone would have had locked such a substantial door, which was unlikely to affected by the wind. To shut it would have been enough, even in this weather. It should be open at all times during a service.

She turned away, feeling as if she had been slapped in the face. She was locked out of her spiritual refuge, left to face the raging storm on her own. Numb with misery and disbelief, she got back into the van and made her way home. This time she made a long detour, not wishing to face the gales on the more exposed dual carriageway now that the stimulus of getting to church was no longer there.

Geoff could see by her face that something was wrong. At first he assumed that she had been involved in an accident. Then she explained that she had been locked out of church, and how upset she was to have made the perilous journey in vain. What she could not explain was how much the church had come to mean to her, how she was more than disappointed. She felt rejected, and told Geoff that she was never going back.

She had been directed to a church that would help her at that stage of her development. Perhaps now she was being directed away, being told that it was time for her to move on. The hurt she felt when she had faced that locked door would take a long time to heal. It was a Spiritualist church. She felt that its doors should always be open during a service. She could not help taking it as a personal insult, and felt that, for some reason, she had been locked out deliberately.

The church president telephoned her a few weeks later. He was concerned because she had not been to church and feared that she might be ill. This caring action was typical of him and of many members of the church. She explained the reason for her absence and he was surprised. He insisted that the door had not been locked during any open circle, either intentionally or accidentally. Amy knew that he was speaking the truth, for he had no reason to lie. Yet she knew that she had done all she could to gain access to the church that night without disrupting the service.

As she became more used to the way that the spirit world influenced her life, Amy realised that they were probably both right. The door had not been locked, yet she had been unable to open it, despite trying more than once. If someone else had arrived late that night they would probably have had no difficulty in entering the church. The door was not closed to them, but it had been closed to Amy. She thought that there must be a reason why she should stay away from the church, so accepted this as being the answer. Perhaps she had reached a stage in her development when she had to do something else. Perhaps she was spending too much time in one place.

During this absence, her probationary membership ended and she received a letter from the church secretary inviting her to become a full member. She wrote back, saying that she no longer wished to become a member of that church.

It was at this time that Amy really missed Pauline. Her down to earth reasoning as they discussed Spiritualism over games of backgammon and her stabilising influence as she made sure that Amy's feet were kept somewhere near the ground. So without Pauline, and the church to lean on, where did she go from here?

The answer to this was nowhere. She had a lot to think about. There was so much to think about at the riding school, which she had intended to pass on to one or both of her daughters. That summer, Susan left school and got a job as stable lass in a National Hunt yard. Teresa had sought this type of employment two years earlier, and neither of them seemed inclined to take over the riding school, which had never got back to what it had been before the miners' strike. Another riding school had recently opened nearby, and there was not enough clientele locally to support them both.

After nine years running the school, Amy found that she had a large amount of capital tied up in ponies and equipment. This was not justified by the returns and she knew that Geoff was capable of making a much better living if he had access to some of that capital. Another reason she was thinking of closing the school was the lack of privacy. Parents tended to use her as an unpaid baby sitter during the school holidays. Some left their children at the stables early in the morning under the pretext that they were 'helping out' and collected them when they came home from work, at tea time. Gradually Amy became over-run with these so-called helpers, who had originally been paying customers, while her actual paying customers dwindled.

She also found that she had to mediate between squabbling girls, or calm angry parents who felt that their child was being picked on by the others. Some parents actually felt that Amy could not have run the school without their daughter's help, and even suggested that she should pay them for the 'work' they did. This unpaid summer camp was something which caused discord both in the stables and within her home, and this upset her.

Finding the right staff was hard, too. Amy was attempting to set up a new business for Geoff, a small antique cum junk shop in a nearby seaside resort. In order to do this she needed to spend time away from the school, so it would be necessary to have a responsible member of staff to run the stable while she was absent. She employed a succession of staff, all of whom, although they themselves were honest, did not protect her from those who were not. They did not care about her property and were careless. Finally, the following year, after three full sized English leather saddles disappeared from the tack room in the space of four months, Amy decided not to renew her licence when it became due at the end of the summer.

She retained Glory and her foals, now aged eight and three, Little Maverick and Bobby. She also allowed some of her livery customers to remain, because their fees helped to subsidise her own horses' keep.

She passed the church every day on her way to and from the shop, but was never tempted to go back. There was no longer an attraction: she had other things to occupy her mind. She had expected to miss the church more than she did, perhaps suffer withdrawal symptoms, now that she no longer had her regular 'fix' of Spiritualism.

The new shop provided them with a modest living from the start, but it was far from what Geoff had made before his brain tumour. Things had changed in the world of antiques and collectables. The popularity of car boot sales had spawned a new generation of 'dealers'. These 'dealers' mainly had other sources of income: most of them had no business ethics, they kept no books, paid no taxes or rates for shop premises. What they did do was provide real competition for their shop. Geoff and Amy found that, in order to survive, they had to join in; sell bric a brac, books and records at flea markets in order to earn a decent living.

It was a relief for them to have the house to themselves when they returned home from the shop. Amy had not realised how much of her life had been taken up with other people's children. At least now her evenings were her own. It was during this period that she realised that she was not the only one in the family who had psychic gifts.

Both of her daughters had shown that they were aware of the old man's spirit, but neither had shown any interest in the church. Susan was educated in a convent, so when her mother began to frequent a Spiritualist church, she had been appalled. Perhaps she had visions of her mother becoming damned beyond all redemption.

Susan did not know her mother's family very well, so Amy was surprised when she began to talk about them after a brief visit to her aunt's house. Amy was giving Susan a lift back to her job, and had called in to see her aunt Alice on the way. When they left, Susan began to talk about her great grandmother, who had died when Susan was two. She began by saying that the grandmother used to overcook cabbage, which left a distinctive smell in the house every Sunday. Surprised, Amy said this was true. Susan then went on to give information about her grandmother which Amy herself had forgotten and later had to confirm with older members of her family.

Susan was talking as if she was recounting memories, and even mentioned the grandmother's second husband's Christian name. This was unusual, because everyone referred to him as 'Jock'. Amy only knew his Christian name because she had seen letters addressed to him.

Amy was careful not to lead Susan on, and answered only 'yes' or 'no'. She realised that Susan was mediumistic and asked if she had thought about developing this. Susan was not interested and was surprised that her mother should suggest such a thing. She was too young to spend her time in a Spiritualist church. That sort of thing was for weirdoes and old women, like her mother.

The shop did very well in its first year of trading. Because of her interest in books, Amy found that she had built up a large stock, too many to be displayed in the shop. When the adjacent shop became empty, she rented it and opened it as a bookshop. Because both of the shops were in a holiday resort and the trade seasonal, they continued to supplement their takings by renting a stall at a local flea market.

Working in the flea market involved an early start and Amy was usually very tired as she packed her books up at the end of the day. All she wanted to do was to get home and put her feet up in front of the television.

Although she had given up the church, she still had experiences at night. She would hear rapping on the headboard, and sometimes she felt as if someone had touched her shoulder, or stroked her hair. She regularly felt 'cobwebs' on her face, which she later found was a sign that spirit people had drawn close to her. Often, when she felt these 'cobwebs', she also experienced static electricity, which literally made her hair stand on end.

Then, one busy afternoon, as she packed up after the flea market, she announced that she was going to church that night. Geoff pointed out that she had said she was never going back. She admitted this, but she was not going to change her mind this time. Whatever he said, she was going to church.

As she got ready, she began to look forward to the service. She had been away almost eighteen months. Things would have changed, she was sure of that, but she knew she had to go. It felt right to go. As she drove to the church she became apprehensive. Would she be able to receive messages, as she had before? What would her reception be, after all this time? She regretted not telephoning the president to test his reaction to her return. All this was running through her mind as she approached the church. With trembling hands, she tried the heavy door. It swung open.

# Chapter Seven

The church president looked up as Amy entered the church. He stopped what he was doing and came to greet her with a broad smile and gave her a bear hug. By the end of the night, others had demonstrated their pleasure in seeing her in a similar manner and she felt as if she had never been away. She knew most of the congregation, although there were a number of faces she did not recognise. Quite a few of the regulars were missing, but Amy thought that it was because most churches have a shifting congregation. Some people sample what a church has to offer then pass on: others use it as and when they need it. That's what the church is there for: to be used.

With a couple of exceptions, the mediums who worked that night were different to those who had worked before she had left the church. There were those who had never given a message, or who had hesitantly stumbled through a communication, who now confidently worked as mediums. She was impressed to see how much they had developed while she had been away.

She did not see any pictures in her mind that night, but she thoroughly enjoyed the service. There was an abundance of mediums, all eager and willing to work: as soon as one sat down, another got to her feet. Amy did not see anything the following week, either. Instead, she found herself looking around the circle, making up stories about people she was drawn to. By the third week, with no pictures appearing in her mind, she was beginning to feel that she had lost the ability to communicate with the spirit world. Then she reasoned that perhaps she was just a little rusty. After all, she had not consciously communicated with spirits during her time away from the church.

Would she have to start from the beginning? Or was it something that you never forgot, like riding a bike? She did not know. Week after week she sat, making up stories, until one night she felt as if she was being pushed to get to her feet. As soon as the floor was clear, she stood up and began to relate to a stranger the story she had 'made up' about her. To Amy's surprise, the woman accepted all she said. When she sat down she felt a warm glow spreading through her chest. This glow was to become a familiar feeling, a sign that Amy had done well with the information she had received.

So why was she not seeing pictures? There is a simple answer. Amy was not communicating visually, or clairvoyantly, but audibly, or clairaudiently. The 'stories' she was making up were thoughts relayed to her mind by the spirit world. Previously, her mind had translated these thoughts to visual images. Now she was experiencing thoughts which were not her own, but meant to be related to others. She had to work this out for herself, for the church regulars were either reluctant to explain this to her or they did not know themselves. She knew there was such a thing as clairaudience, for she had read Doris Stokes' books. However, she had thought that clairaudience meant that she would hear voices in her ear, as Doris had implied.

It would have been a simple matter for one of the mediums in the church to explain this to her, but they either did not recognise what was happening to her, or they were not prepared to give her the benefit of their experience and knowledge. Amy did not realise that, if she wanted to gain knowledge she would have to conform to what those who were in charge of the church thought was right. This included following a pattern and timetable which they felt was a universal formula for developing mediums. She tried to do this, but felt restrained and was literally champing at the bit to learn more. Surely they could see that people are individuals: each developing at a different speed.

Her mediumship had developed during her absence from the church. Her confidence had grown and she was becoming more accurate in pinpointing the recipient of any message she received. While she sorted out her material problems, someone in the spirit world, probably her spirit guide, had helped her to develop without her being aware of doing so. Perhaps he had done this while she was asleep, or in a similar receptive state.

She did feel that she was progressing, but still thought that there was something was missing. She had no idea who her spirit guide was. She was not aware of ever having seen him, or of being able to recognise him from other spirits. She thought he might have been the spirit whom she had sent away from her bedside. If this was so, would he ever come back? Or perhaps he was the monk she had seen at the séance? These questions remained unanswered and she felt inadequate when she heard others in the church relating conversations they had had with their guides and referring to them by name. How could she be a proper medium if she did not know who her guide was?

Amy's sister had given her three Doris Stokes books, thinking that they would be of some help. However, Doris was a natural medium and had been clairvoyant and clairaudient from an early age, so there was not a lot in these books to which Amy could relate. They had nothing in them which would help her to establish the identity of her guide. Doris referred to many conversations with her own guide and this confused Amy. Was there something she was neglecting to do? Had she not reached the stage where she could distinguish her guide from other spirits? Did she have a guide? If not, how did she get one? You cannot buy them in a shop, or order them by mail order. These were the thoughts running through Amy's mind as she struggled with this problem.

At this point, although she attended regularly, she had not rejoined the church. She did not feel that she was ready for such a commitment, but was happy to help with any fundraising and attend as many of their services as she could. She had begun to feel that perhaps she would not be welcomed as a member, or that she might not fit in. She always felt as if she was kept on the outside looking in and she was not sure that church membership would change this. There seemed to be a nucleus of people who mattered, a sort of inner circle, and the rest were there just to make up the numbers. Long standing members of the church often left, never to return, because of disagreements and changes in this inner circle. This worried Amy. She took a step backwards for a while and tried to look at the church from a wider angle. She realised that a church is made up of people, all of whom made mistakes. There are always personality clashes in any group and these were sensitive people who took things to heart. In every group there are also those who refuse to admit that they can make, or have made, a mistake. The problem starts when these people take control.

In order to raise funds, the church held coffee mornings once a month. As well as various stalls, three mediums would attend and give private sittings. These sittings were always in great demand, and so Amy never booked one for herself. She did not feel that she needed one. She had all the evidence she could ever need: something she could hold in her hand whenever she doubted. The horseshoe travelled everywhere with her in her handbag because she had not got around to hanging it on the wall.

At one of these coffee mornings she was told that there was a vacant sitting because someone had cancelled. Rather than let the church lose the money from the sitting, Amy decided to take it. She did not know the medium and had never seen her work, although the woman had a good reputation. The medium took Amy's hands in hers and closed her eyes for a moment. She began to tell Amy about family and friends who had passed over. Then the medium became serious.

*"I feel you have been through a lot in your life,"* she said, *"You have used these experiences to learn. You will do great work for the church one day."*

Amy opened her mouth to speak, intending to tell the woman that she was already working in the open circle, then remembered that she was not supposed to 'feed' the medium with information. She nodded, thinking that this woman meant that one day she would take church services. She wanted to tell her that she had no ambition to do this, but then the medium said something which was to change Amy's life.

*"This movement is desperately short of ambassadors,"* she said. *"That is where your work will lie."*

The medium had chosen one of the few words which would interest Amy. She had never been able to visualise herself as a working medium, but becoming an ambassador was different. It appealed to her ego. Yes, she felt she could definitely see herself becoming an ambassador!

She left the sitting, sought out the membership secretary, paid a subscription and rejoined the church as an associate member. She did not know how to begin to be an ambassador, but knew that if she did manage to become one, she would do the job well. She had always wanted to help the church in some way. Now she had a goal to aim at. She knew she had a gift and that it should be developed to a higher standard so that she had control over it. She wanted to understand this gift, to know how she was obtaining these messages, and who it was who gave them to her. She did not want to be a tool used by a nameless, faceless spirit. Once again she turned for advice to the more experienced members of the church.

The president was very patient with her, but he was not in the best of health, so she hesitated in making demands on his time. He gave so much of it to the church and she felt guilty in monopolising him. The president's wife always gave her sound advice. She never attempted to influence Amy with her personal views, but gave her the benefit of her experience. Unfortunately, this well meaning woman's knowledge was not extensive, and she was virtually the only one willing to help Amy. Others, who could have helped, sat back and watched as Amy groped her way forward in the dark. They never offered to help, or commended her when she did well, but were quick to criticise when she made mistakes.

It was about this time that Amy wondered if her mediumship was improving, or if she was merely too familiar with the congregation and was relaying information about them that was stored in her subconscious mind. There was one way to find out. She could go to another church, and see if she could work in their open circle. She decided to go back to the church which she had visited with Pauline, reasoning that if she was able work in that cold, cheerless place she could assume that she really was communicating with the 'other side'. Another reason she chose that church was that it was the only other Spiritualist church that she knew.

From the moment she opened the door she felt the church had changed. She was welcomed by a pleasant young man.

*"Good evening,"* he said, handing her a hymn book, *"May I ask if this is your first visit to a Spiritualist church?"*

Amy replied that she usually attended another church and they chatted for a while before going into the room where the services were held. The atmosphere in the room was different to what it had been on her previous visit, and there had been many improvements. It had been redecorated, refurbished and was brighter in every way. The chairs were now placed in a large circle and she felt at home from the start. Even so, she wished that Pauline was with her.

As she waited for the service to start, she began to feel apprehensive. How could she work in a strange church when she did not know the identity of her guide? As the service began, she was full of misgivings. Was she really there to test herself, or was she on an ego trip? Either way, her confidence began to flag. Her only consolation was that she was a stranger to these people. If she made a fool of herself it would not matter. She could walk away and not return.

The service was dominated by a woman who appeared to be determined that the floor should be occupied at all times. She mentioned that if anyone wished to give a message they should signal to her by raising their hand. Amy suppressed a desire to giggle. If Pauline had been with her she would probably have done so. It was a bit like being back at school. The woman seemed intent on staying on her feet. When she was not actually giving a message, she stood in the middle of the circle with her eyes closed in an attempt to get another communication. Consequently, it was very difficult for anyone to attract her attention without interrupting her.

The woman fascinated Amy, who was very happy to sit and observe her work. Now and then Amy tried to meditate, but found that she was listening to what was being said. Then she had the feeling that she was being pushed off her seat. Eventually, she managed to get the woman's attention and was allowed to stand up.

The communication she gave was accepted, much to her relief, and she felt the now familiar warm glow creep over her. She gave another communication that night and felt that she had proven to herself that she was able to work outside her own church. If this was so, then she must be getting the information she relayed from somewhere.

Amy did not tell anyone at her own church that she had visited another open circle in case someone commented on it. A few weeks later the president announced that the church would be holding three classes. The first would be for beginners, the second an awareness class, and the third, a development class. The third class took Amy's eye. Its purpose was to develop mediumship. It was just what she had been waiting for.

She was soon made aware that many church members thought that she should consider joining one of the other classes. They considered that she was aiming too high and would be out of her depth in the development class. She hesitated, feeling that she should wait before making up her mind. Perhaps there was truth in what they were saying. Was she really ready for such a big step forward? After all, she did not even know who her spirit guide was. In the end she decided to wait until nearer to the deadline before choosing which class to join.

The president's wife was helpful, as usual. She suggested that Amy should prepare for the class by learning to meditate. She explained that regular meditation would help her to become more aware of her spirit helpers and guides. Amy set aside a half an hour every night, after Geoff had gone to bed, for meditation.

She found it very difficult. The dogs, particularly Tim, jumped onto her knee as soon as she sat down. She tried to lock them in the morning room, but they cried and scratched at the door. Eventually, she taught them that they had to stay quietly on the settee while she meditated in Geoff's armchair. She found it hard to relax, expecting that at any moment one of them would decide to jump onto her lap. She also found difficulty in clearing her mind and she would think of things which had happened during the day, or things she had to do tomorrow. However, practice makes perfect and gradually her thinking (and worrying) time grew shorter while her meditation grew longer. Even the dogs learned to respect that this was time that she needed for herself and they settled happily on the settee. They must have watched her closely, because moment she opened her eyes they raced, growling at each other, as they positioned themselves in what they considered to be their rightful spot, her lap.

During these meditations, Amy began to feel someone, whom she presumed to be her guide, coming close to her. She knew he was there, but was still no nearer to identifying him. Soon she began to see colours, and sometimes, pictures, in her mind. One night she saw the most beautiful colours, ranging from pink to lilac, then a deep purple. She felt relaxed and at peace with herself when she finished meditating, and when she went to bed she thought that it was a pity she did not know who had brought these colours. She would have liked to have been able to acknowledge him, and thank him for the peace she had felt and the beauty he had shown her.

She closed her eyes for a moment as she sat on her bed. Immediately, her mind was filled with the picture of a Native American with a full headdress. He seemed to be very strong, and looked wise and noble. She felt that he had been a great man, one who had learned much during his physical life. She felt privileged to have him as her guide, yet in the back of her mind she was a little disappointed. Everyone seemed to have a Native American guide. It was so common, and she had felt that she would have been different.

She slept well and soundly that night, and the first thing she thought of the next day was that she knew the identity of her spirit guide. She had not given him a name, for she had not been inspired to, but she was glad to know who was with her. She could not wait to tell someone, and chose Ben, a young man who sometimes played the piano in church. He was glad to hear that she had seen this man, for he knew how seriously she took her development. However, he was not convinced that the man she had seen was her guide.

*"I think you will find that this man is your door keeper,"* he said, *"I don't want to put ideas in your head about your guide, but I've always been aware that you have someone with you and he is not a Native American."*

Amy was disappointed and a little deflated, having got a different reaction from Ben than she had expected. How could he say this? He had not seen him. If he knew who her guide was, then he should tell her. She felt that the Native American had to be her guide, otherwise, why had she seen him? The shine had gone off her discovery, and she decided not to tell anyone else. Still, she was happy that she had seen the Native American. Now she felt that she was a proper medium. Armed with this belief, she put her name on the list for the development class.

She had only just beaten the deadline, for the list was taken down the following Sunday. Eyebrows were raised when her name appeared on the list and there was a lot of comment. Some did not say anything, but their silent disapproval spoke volumes. Others made no attempt to hide the fact that they felt she was not ready for such a class. They intimated that she had not been in the church for two minutes, and thought she knew it all. Whatever the president's wife felt, she kept to herself. Amy knew that without this good lady's help, she would never have felt ready to join the class.

Ben was not overjoyed when he found she was joining the class, but did not attempt to put her off. He advised her to take what she could from the class and look upon it as a learning experience which would be a valuable part of her development. Whatever she felt that she could not accept, she should not reject, but hold on to it, for there would be a time when she had learned enough to understand it. He did not wish to influence her, only to help her to get the most out of what she had decided to do. Armed with this advice, she looked forward to her first class.

# Chapter Eight

It is no wonder that Spiritualism is not accepted by many major religions. A lot of the problems encountered by Spiritualism is self inflicted and originate within itself. There are people who call themselves Spiritualists who enjoy making Spiritualism seem like a mystical secret. Perhaps they feel that this makes them stand out in a crowd because they are different, special and mystical. Newcomers and other uninformed people are expected to hang on their every word and treat them with awe. Whenever Amy asked about the development class, she was met with pursed lips, headshaking and warnings that whatever went on in the development circle was a secret, not to be discussed with all and sundry. They made it sound like a secret society which Amy should have felt honoured to be allowed to join. Consequently, she was confused and apprehensive when she attended her first class.

The first evening was in the form of a 'get to know you' session. All but four of the sitters were members of the church and everyone was more experienced than Amy. They all knew what to expect and were looking forward to starting work. Amy decided that it would be prudent to observe the others, and say as little as possible. She felt very much as if she was in the 'A' level stream without having done the groundwork, but knew that she would learn more in this class than she had been able to glean from all the questions she had asked since coming to the church. These people all had the same aim: to work together for their mutual development. Because of this, there was a feeling of harmony within the circle.

Amy had never shirked from a challenge and was usually seen at her best when she was being extended. She had never enjoyed being a big fish in a small pool, which was just as well, for she was a minnow among dolphins in this class. They would certainly push her to her limits.

She had been warned that by joining the circle, she would be committing herself to attending every class. The only excuse for absence would be illness or holidays. She had no problem with this commitment, and made sure that she was never absent because she felt she could not afford to miss even one class. Luckily, she was rarely ill and holidays were not a problem, because she could not afford one. This was the first opportunity she had been given to learn and she did not intend to waste it. She knew there was a chance that she would not be able to keep up with the others and be asked to leave. She hoped that if this happened, she would be able to leave with her dignity intact. It is difficult to admit you are wrong, and Amy knew she would not be the first person ever to become over ambitious. It is human to seek that which attracts you rather than to accept that which is right for you.

When the introductions were completed, each member of the class was asked to describe themselves briefly and to state their reason for joining the class. Amy was second to go.

*"I joined this class because I have found a lot of peace and happiness since I came into Spiritualism,"* she began. *"I want to share this with others, but nobody wants to listen to you unless you are an accomplished clairvoyant. I hope to improve my clairvoyance in this class."*

As the others gave their reasons for joining the class, Amy began to feel that her reason had seemed childlike and selfish in comparison.

Time was to prove that sitting with this group was exactly what she needed. They were keen to help, and, although there were times when Amy felt she was holding them back, this charge was never laid at her door. What she did not know at the time was that five of the most experienced sitters were there to help the rest of the class to develop. Four of these, made up of two couples, travelled a long way just to help the novices, and Amy will always be grateful to them.

The circle leader, Joseph, was a young man half Amy's age, and at that time was one of the most sought after mediums in the area. He had a tremendous energy and capacity for work, and he expected his class to be the same. Despite his tender years, he seemed to Amy to have a great deal of knowledge and experience. What is more important is that he was prepared to pass this knowledge on to others. As with most talented people, he had his critics. Before Amy joined the class she was warned that Joseph's temper was short and that patience was not one of his virtues. She was also warned that the class would be forced, like rhubarb in a bucket, and shoot away quickly without absorbing much knowledge. Luckily, Amy prefers to make up her own mind, and judges people by their performance rather than their reputation. If she had followed the advice, so freely given, she would not have benefited from the teachings and fellowship of the circle.

Amy had stated that she had wanted to improve her psychic ability, but she was also seeking answers. She needed to know where she was going, and why. She was aware that there was another way she had to grow, but was not certain what it was. Actions speak louder than words, and Amy realised that she had to practice what she preached if she was to become an ambassador for Spiritualism. The more she learned, the more capable she was of learning, and things she had not understood before were now beginning to make sense. She had added another dimension to her thinking, allowing her to look at life from a much wider angle, and see things she had not noticed before. It was as if her mind had been a dormant seed, content to lie in the darkness and comfort of familiar things.

A development circle is like a greenhouse, where the seeds are given all they need to grow: the right conditions, proper food, care and encouragement. There is a great deal of difference between forced rhubarb and a carefully cultivated plant. The experienced members of the circle acted as gardeners, helping the others through the trauma of their growth. The class operated in a controlled environment, similar to a greenhouse, given time to 'harden off' until ready to go out into the garden of life. If they then passed on a little of what they had learned, it would be the fruits of the whole class, not just their own.

Joseph was a strict disciplinarian, demanding the same standards from the class as he set himself. Contrary to the tales she had heard, Amy found that he could be patient, and he always made sure that they understood the lesson before going on to the next. I am not saying that she always agreed with him, because that would not be true. There were even times when they argued until they had to agree to differ. She had no intention of becoming a clone of a successful medium, and on one occasion she told him this in no uncertain terms. What did happen was that they built up a mutual respect for each other.

On one occasion they were each asked to describe their spirit guide. Because she was sitting on Joseph's left, Amy had to go first. She normally dreaded being the first, because she liked to see the others work before she attempted an exercise herself. However, she was pleased to go first on this occasion, because she knew she could do this. After all, she had seen her guide, hadn't she? His image was as clear in her mind today as when she had first seen him. She stood up, and began to describe, in great detail, the Native American.

*"That's enough,"* interrupted Joseph. *"Dave, describe Amy's guide."*

Dave was sitting directly opposite Amy. As he stood up, she sat down, feeling confused.

*"Your guide,"* Dave began, *"is a literary gentleman who lived during the Victorian era."*

He continued, describing someone that Amy had never consciously been aware of, yet at the same time, seemed very familiar to her. He was describing someone whom Amy had known all her life.

Amy wondered how she was unable to see her guide when others were able to do so. She was also worried that the class may have thought that she had made up the Native American, for wasn't he everyone's idea of a spirit guide? Later, she asked Joseph why she had seen him, if he was not her guide. Joseph explained that she would have many helpers and inspirers who would work with her during her lifetime. The Native American was one, and when she had expressed a desire to see who was working with her that particular evening, he had shown himself. She had not asked to see her guide, just the communicator. This made sense to Amy, and she accepted it, remembering that Ben had previously told her that the Native American was not her guide, but her doorkeeper.

This new discovery made her want to know more. The revelation that her guide had been a literary gentleman made sense. She had been a prolific writer since the age of ten and she always got top marks for essays and compositions at school. Poetry and prose flowed easily through her pen throughout the time she was at school. Even now, in her hectic life, she was often inspired to put her thoughts on paper.

She was determined to get to know her guide. She realised now that she had probably felt his presence, but had been unable to distinguish him from the Native American or other spirit helpers. She thought that she was not advanced enough to do this, or perhaps the time was not right, but she was determined that she would do her very best to get closer to him. Then one night, during a meditation in the class, she saw the outline of a man who seemed vaguely familiar. His face was blurred, and when she tried to bring it into focus he disappeared.

For the first time she felt she had to attach a name to this man, and mentally asked him what his name was. She was not aware of any reply. Determined not to let this opportunity slip away, she decided to name him herself.

*"Then I shall call you Henry,"* she said, in her mind, then felt as if she had committed a breach of etiquette. Should she be so familiar? Then she felt him speak.

*"Mr. Latimer, if you please."*

Now she knew his name! She was successfully communicating with her guide! She could hardly wait to get to the end of the exercise to tell the others. Dave, especially was pleased, and he mentioned that her guide was a cockney.

As soon as he said this Amy knew he was wrong, for in her mind, she heard Mr. Latimer say. *"I was not a cockney. I was born in Hammersmith."*

She was puzzled. How could she know this, other than by receiving information from her guide? As soon as Dave had spoken, the reply came into her mind. This was to happen regularly, and she soon realised that this was the way Mr. Latimer communicated with her. As soon as she asked a question, or was asked one by someone else, the answer flashed into her mind.

Amy entered into a period of getting to know her guide. She experimented with writing, something she had not attempted for some time. The words flowed, and she knew she was receiving at least part of what she wrote from Mr. Latimer. The most important thing was that she felt that she liked him, and could identify with him. She realised that she could have done so much more with her life if she had been aware of him sooner. Now they were communicating: they made a good team, and she was so pleased that he was her guide.

He was eloquent, and influenced her whenever she allowed him to do so. She also began to understand what she was being taught, and because of this, she progressed rapidly. She found that, if she was stuck for words, she could take a deep breath, and allow Mr. Latimer to help her. His words always made more sense.

She could not wait to see Ben, who was pleased that she had found out the identity of her guide. He listened with great interest then said something that she had not thought of.

*"If Mr. Latimer lived during the Victorian era, you may be able to find out more about him in the records. It's a pity you don't know where he lived."*

The name of a street flashed into her mind, and she told Ben. He suggested that she should look in the London A-Z, to see if there was such a street in Hammersmith, which she did as soon as she got home. She scanned through the index, and was disappointed to find that there was no street of that name in Hammersmith, or any other part of London. She had become so used to the information she was receiving being right, that she could hardly believe it. She felt that she must have made a mistake somewhere along the line, so began to look at the street maps, using Hammersmith as a base then moving outwards.

On the outskirts of Hammersmith, possibly even in the neighbouring borough, she found a street which was only two letters different from the street she was looking for. More importantly, it sounded the same. Satisfied that her information could be correct after all, she decided that, when she had time, she would begin to look for Mr. Latimer. More than fifteen years has passed since then, and she has not seriously attempted this search.

As Amy began to get to know her guide she began to feel very close to him. She felt inspired to write again, and was conscious that there were times when he influenced her thoughts as she wrote. In the past she had written many stories and articles, only to leave them unfinished, to gather dust, or be relegated to the back of a drawer. Mr. Latimer gave her the discipline to finish what she began, and the patience to start over again when she realised that she had gone wrong. Time flies when you're having fun, and all too soon it was time to break for the Christmas holidays.

That Christmas was a good one. Both of the shops had done well, and Amy had no worries about money. On Christmas Eve she went into the market to buy a fresh goose, because Geoff did not eat turkey. In previous years they had killed their own, or attended the poultry auctions, but this year they had been too busy, so Amy found herself in town on the busiest day of the year.

She bought a good fat goose, and on her way to the car park she passed a flower stall. She did not normally buy flowers for the house at Christmas, but, even though she was heavily laden, she stopped to look at the stall. A thought came to her. She would buy flowers for everyone she knew who was in the spirit world. She chose a large mixed bouquet, and started to walk away. Then she went back for more. These were for all the souls in the spirit world who had nobody to buy flowers for them. As she walked away a warm glow spread through her, and she knew that Mr. Latimer approved.

That evening, when all the work was done, she settled down to watch television with Geoff. The flowers gave her a lot of pleasure. As she looked at them, her thoughts went to her grandmother and the Christmas memories they had shared together. She felt that she should have bought roses, as they shared a special memory of roses at Christmas, but she knew that her grandmother would not mind.

Her thoughts strayed to Mr. Latimer, and she wondered how he would have celebrated Christmas. What kind of flowers would he have liked? As soon as she had thought this, he replied.

*"Gardenia."*

She had no idea what a gardenia looked like, but decided to visit a flower shop after the holidays to see if she could buy one. When she asked the florist, he was surprised.

*"I do have one,"* he said, *"But I shouldn't have it."*

He explained that he'd had a delivery of gardenia for a special order, and had come in early that morning to water all the plants before delivering the order. On his return, his assistant held up a gardenia plant and asked what it was doing in the back shop. The florist had been puzzled, because he had watered every plant in the shop, and this gardenia was dry.

*"So you see,"* he said, *"I don't know how it managed to escape. It might have been behind something else, but I can't think how, because the gardenias were delivered to us in a tray and I delivered them to my customer in the same tray."*

As he related the story, Amy could not resist smiling. She knew it was not strange. She also felt that Mr. Latimer had saved the gardenia for her.

*"It's funny the way it happened,"* the florist continued. *"I don't have much call for gardenia and I only bought them for that special order, then you come along and ask for one."*

Mr. Latimer's gardenia proved difficult to keep. It needed a constant, warm, humid atmosphere, and the draughty old farmhouse, despite its central heating, was not the right environment. Amy bought a few gardenia plants after that, but was not successful with them until she moved house.

When the class resumed after the Christmas break, Joseph informed them that they would be working hard and taking a large step up. They had to learn about presentation, how to make themselves heard and how to deal with problems during a service. Working on the rostrum of a Spiritualist church has its pitfalls. There are often newcomers in the congregation who are not sure what to expect, or how to respond to the medium. They may be mourning the loss of a loved one. Perhaps they are unable to come to terms with their bereavement, so turn to the Spiritualist church in the hope they will receive news that their loved ones have survived their physical death. These people often expect to hear only from the person they are mourning, and can reject any other spirit who comes forward.

Mediums cannot demand the spirit world to supply specific information, or ask for one particular spirit to come forward. They are only the instrument used to connect the two sides of life, and can only relay what is given to them.

Other problems the class had to learn to overcome were people who talk during the service, those who rustle sweet wrappers, or rattle their small change as they sort out their contribution to the collection. Lastly, they learned how to cope with sceptics and those who, for various reasons, want the medium to fail.

Class members were expected to be able to take any part of the service. This included the prayers which open and close the service. To her horror, Amy found that she could not pray in public. She had no problem with personal prayers, but found herself stuck for words when expected to stand up in the circle and say the opening or closing prayer. Because of this weakness, Joseph made sure that Amy was given every opportunity to open or close in prayer.

One night he asked Eileen, one of the other sitters, to begin the closing prayer. Amy was instructed to listen carefully, and when Eileen sat down Amy was to finish the prayer. Normally a closing prayer is short, but this one was not. Eileen did a magnificent job, and everyone was entranced by the beauty of the prayer. Whenever she hesitated, Amy got ready to stand up, but she went on again. It was such a spiritual prayer that Amy felt that she would never be able to do it justice. Then Eileen sat down. Amy stood up. She knew what the perfect ending for the prayer would be.

*"Amen."* she said.

Joseph's bowed head jerked for a moment, and he raised it to look at her. She quaked in her shoes. Surely she was in trouble. Then, slowly, a smile crept across his face, much to the relief of the whole circle, who had wanted to laugh, but dared not do so in case they, too, incurred his wrath.

*"Yes,"* he said. *"It was complete, wasn't it?"*

Occasionally the class went as a group to other churches to work in their open circles. At first Amy was not sure that she could work under Joseph's critical eye, but she found it easier than working in her own church. She felt happier giving messages to strangers, for she knew that she could not possibly be drawing on her knowledge of their lives.

The thought of standing on the rostrum still worried Amy. She did not see a light moving from one person to another, and she did not see spirits other than in her mind. However, she did have faith in her guide and was confident that he would never let her down. She wished she could see him, but he remained illusive. She hoped that she would progress to a stage where she would see spirits, including Mr. Latimer, but knew that this might never happen. Better mediums than her had gone into the spirit world without ever seeing spirit other than in their mind, as she did. She felt that Mr. Latimer would one day show himself to her, but it did not matter. She knew he was there.

One night, as she was settling down to sleep, she heard someone call her name. The voice was loud, and seemed to come out of her ear. It was so loud, in fact, that she felt that Geoff must surely have heard it, too. He had not. She waited to see if the voice would come again. Then, as soon as she relaxed, she heard it again. Too late, she realised that she should have spoken to the voice when she'd first heard it. Now she was tired and wanted to go to sleep. She said this to the spirit and heard nothing more that night.

The class was progressing really well, and Amy felt that things were really happening for her. If only they could have remained that way. But no man is an island. The class had to exist among people, some of whom were neither pleased nor impressed at the way the novices were progressing. Some of the class began to experience difficulty when working in the open circle, and more than one complained of headaches afterwards. Joseph attended the open circle and explained to the class that the reason they were having problems was that someone was 'blocking' them.

Amy could not understand why anyone would do such a thing. Perhaps they felt threatened by the developing mediums. Joseph showed them how to counteract this interference. They were shown how to reach a little higher, to work on a vibration that these people cannot reach when they are 'blocking'. They would be working psychically and on a very low level.

Amy wondered why the spirit world allowed people do this. She thought about it, and watched. Then she realised that everyone who attends a Spiritualist church is not necessarily a Spiritualist. They regard Spiritualism as a hobby rather than a way of life, treating developing mediums as rivals and are suspicious of anyone who acts in a truly spiritual manner. They devote as much time as they can to their hobby, pursuing it with the zeal of true enthusiasts, but failing to grasp that Spiritualism is a way of life, not a pastime. The church may mean a lot to these people and they may reach a position of power. Seeing others develop or taking an active role in the church worries them, and they feel threatened. Instead of going forward themselves, they take the retrograde step of attempting (and sometimes, succeeding) to discredit those whom they see as rivals. Amy worked on the principle that success without honour is failure. Any position achieved in life should be justly deserved and gained without causing grief to others. Holding others back does not make us into better people.

Eventually, if those who wish to remain big fish in a small pool are allowed to continue to pollute the waters, others have to leave in order to be able to breath. Amy was to learn the hard way that when this happens you have to learn to let go. By remaining you contribute to the pollution, as your very presence causes more offence to those who are determined that you should go. In the following years she found it increasingly difficult to remain. She asked her inspirers what she should do, and they answered. *"Join the rest of the little fish, head for the ocean: feed on the truth that Spiritualism offers and you will grow."*

# Chapter Nine

There was much more to being a medium than Amy had previously realised. The class was taught a little of the history and philosophy of Spiritualism, as well as how the phenomena associated with Spiritualism worked. As a medium she would be expected to be able to answer questions put to her by members of the public. She devoured this information, and the more she learned, the more she realised how much rubbish she had been fed in the past.

I would like to say that the rubbish had been fed to her by non Spiritualists, but this was not true. Amy would be the first to admit that she had had preconceived ideas about Spiritualism before joining the movement. This was due to ignorance, or to listening to those who professed knowledge, yet were only repeating what they had learned from others. Some of this had been based on supposition, or opinions, and was rarely based on knowledge acquired through courses and literature available through the Spiritualist movement.

Even today, there are still misguided people within Spiritualism who give credence to these inaccuracies. Indeed, they are sometimes responsible for them. Spiritualism has dragged itself into the twenty first century, gradually shaking off these myths, which cling like limpets to its sides. Its job is made difficult by those who perpetuate myths and half truths, breeding more limpets to hinder the progress of the movement.

These people feel that the more mystical and mysterious Spiritualism sounds, the more important they themselves appear to others. They do not attempt to further their own education, but are content with what they feel they know. Their minds remain closed, resistant to the drive by others to encourage education within the movement.

Old wives' tales thread their way through Spiritualism like bindweed through a garden. How can the newcomer recognise the difference between truth and half truth: between weed and cultivated plant? A novice gardener might well accept bindweed into his garden, and fail to eliminate it. He may even, in his ignorance, cultivate it and pass cuttings on to other less knowledgeable gardeners. Likewise, there are those who give credence to untruths and half truths that they have been taught as facts. They subsequently pass them on, and so the misinformation is spread.

Usually, an old wives' tale starts as someone's observation. This might be picked up and repeated until it is accepted as an unwritten law. There are too many examples of this within Spiritualism, and Amy never ceased to be surprised at the number of people who actually believed them. One of the most repeated myths was the idea that, unless a medium was a bundle of nerves before a service, then he/she was on an ego trip. Those who knew more than Amy all agreed that this was the case, so she naturally assumed that she, too, would suffer an attack of nerves once she began to take services.

She was confused when she had no suck attack as she prepared to join the class in taking a service which had been arranged by Joseph. The others made a big show of being nervous. Some even said that they felt that they wanted to be sick. Amy waited for the butterflies, but none came, nor did she feel sick. On the contrary, she felt very calm, almost numb. She was horrified at her apparent unconcern about the service and too ashamed to admit to the others that she felt fine.

She was glad to get home after the service. Was it possible that she really was on an ego trip? If this was the case she felt that she did not want to go on, because she would be developing for the wrong reasons. Then she realised that the only person likely to give her the answer was her guide. She would ask Mr. Latimer. As she sat quietly in Geoff's chair that night, she sent out her thoughts to her guide, and she received this reply.

*"You will drive many miles to serve churches. If you were to be nervous you would preoccupied and be a danger to yourself and to anyone who had the misfortune to be on the road at the same time. By being nervous, it would suggest that you believed that the service was a performance by you, rather than a co-operation between yourself and those of us who help you. It would also suggest that you lacked faith in your inspirers."*

Because she had treated the old wives' tales as truth, she almost gave up before she started. Since then she has tried not to enforce her opinions on anyone. What was right for her may not be right for the rest of the class, but that does not mean that any of them were wrong. What would be wrong would be to make everyone conform to something which does not apply to them. To pass on your knowledge and observations is one thing, but to lay down your opinions as law is totally unacceptable.

Amy had learned a valuable lesson and in the process had found that Mr. Latimer could help her in many ways. Whenever she ran out of words in a prayer, or talk during a class, Joseph taught her to take a deep breath, and allow her guide to help her. She was surprised that it worked so well. Knowing that she could always rely on help from Joseph, or her spirit inspirers, gave her confidence. Her inspirers were always there, a 'back up' team, ready to help. All she had to do was ask.

Every member of the class was expected to meditate at home for fifteen to twenty minutes each night. They were advised to find some music to meditate to. The only specification for this music was that it had to last twenty minutes at the most. Because her shop sold second hand records as well as books, Amy was spoilt for choice. Where did she begin to look? She felt that big bands, rock music and jazz were not suitable, so began to search through the classical section. This narrowed her search to seven hundred or so long playing records.

As she flipped through them, glancing at the gaudy covers, most of them depicting scenes from opera, she wondered where she could start. What would Mr. Latimer have chosen? As she thought about his possible taste in music, she was drawn to a plain black and green cover with four stringed instruments outlined in white on the black half. It was a recording of a stringed quartet and clarinet playing Mozart's Quintet for clarinet and strings in a major. It was the first, and only, record she tried, and she knew immediately that it was music that she and Mr. Latimer could enjoy together. She selected two pieces, starting with one, then the second, then back to the first, in a musical sandwich. They lasted seventeen minutes in total, just the right length for her home meditation.

The circle had been running for just over a year when the two couples who had devoted their time and energies to helping the developing mediums attended less frequently, then left. Their task was completed: the class was well on its way. Then Joseph announced that he was leaving the area to study for a course connected with his work, and would not be able to continue with the class. His mother, Beth, would take over as circle leader.

Beth was the fifth person who had joined the class to help the novices develop. During the time they had spent together in the class, she had become friends with Amy. Beth often 'linked in' with her while they meditated in their own homes. Although they were four miles apart, Amy could swear that Beth was in the same room as her.

The development class only lasted a matter of months after Joseph left, and Amy was disappointed with this. However, Pauline came home for a visit, and that compensated a little. They spent a lot of time together, catching up with what had happened while they had been apart. Pauline's interest in Spiritualism had grown, and she was eager to go to church. She was also impressed by the way Amy had progressed during her absence, and asked if she would teach her to meditate. Pauline spent long, tedious hours off duty in Saudi Arabia, and felt that by meditating she might be able to reach out to her own guide, and develop spiritually. Amy was pleased to have company, and invited Pauline to join her that evening.

She knew that a person who led a circle had to have certain qualifications. To begin with, they had to be strong. Amy was not clear in what way she would have to be 'strong', but reasoned that this was not really a circle, they were just a couple of friends wanting to meditate together. Surely she could manage that without needing to be supervised.

They had to wait until Geoff went to bed, which was not easy because he felt that it would be ill mannered to leave while they had company. Amy tried to explain that Pauline was not company, she was a friend, and they had lots of things to catch up on. Still he hesitated, so Amy got out the backgammon board and set it up on the coffee table. The two friends had only played three games when Geoff said goodnight and went to bed.

Like naughty schoolgirls having a midnight feast, they giggled and joked as they arranged the furniture and set the tape recorder for their meditation. Amy decided that she would not meditate herself, but would talk Pauline through a guided meditation, using the knowledge she had gained in the class. She began by opening in prayer. They were using Mr. Latimer's music, and Amy felt him very close as she guided Pauline through the meditation. As the music neared the end she asked Pauline to come back to the circle and to open her eyes. After a few moments, Pauline's eyes fluttered then opened.

*"Are you O.K?"* asked Amy. Pauline nodded. *"How do you feel?"* asked Amy.

*"Wonderful,"* replied Pauline. *"I could see everything you described, and went everywhere you took me. It was a beautiful experience."*

Amy felt that Pauline looked bemused, as if she was preoccupied with something. Perhaps she had a communication, and did not realise what to do.

*"Have you got something to say to me?"* she asked.

*"What do you mean?"* asked Pauline.

*"Take a deep breath, and say the first thing that comes into your mind,"* advised Amy.

Pauline took a deep breath, and her head rolled back. Before Amy could say or do anything, an ectoplasmic mask appeared in front of Pauline's face. A face of a woman appeared, pressed into the mask. Before Amy could recognise the face, another appeared, then a succession of faces, each lasting a matter of seconds before fading and disappearing.

Amy knew that she should remain calm, but it was difficult, because she was confused. This had never happened during her development circle. She was fascinated by the faces and wanted to see more, but knew that she should bring Pauline back. For a moment she was torn between watching the faces and calling her friend back to the circle. Then she called Pauline's name, trying to sound calm and in control. Pauline did not respond, so Amy called again, telling her she must come back. Then she asked Mr. Latimer to help, and called again.

*"Pauline, you must come back to the circle."*

As suddenly as it had appeared, the mask melted away. Pauline opened her eyes, and looked dazed. Amy asked her if she was all right, and she nodded.

*"I'll close in prayer, then."* said a relieved Amy, anxious to make sure that Pauline did not go off again.

Over a cup of coffee, Pauline described how she had felt while she was transfiguring. She described being in a dark place, similar to a tunnel: she could not see or touch the walls or ceiling, but felt that it was tubular, like a gigantic pipe. She could only remember hearing Amy call her back twice, whereas she had been called at least five or six times. She was not aware that she had been used to display the faces of spirit people who had come forward to be recognised.

Amy was annoyed with herself for not paying more attention to the faces, or trying to put a name to any of them. She had been torn between watching the faces and looking after Pauline. Amy wondered if Pauline might be capable of physical mediumship, but at that point in time her knowledge was insufficient to make a proper judgement.

Physical mediums, those who are able to produce physical phenomena, (transfiguration, materialisation, direct voice and table tilting, to name but a few,) are rare. They have to be developed over a long period of time, usually many years, and normally only work in closed circles. Amy had seen a couple of public demonstrations of transfiguration, but had never been impressed. What she had seen with Pauline had surpassed anything she has seen before or since. The faces had seemed real. They were three dimensional, with great detail, not like the blurred images she had witnessed in the public demonstrations.

Pauline's experience rekindled her interest, and she voiced an ambition to learn more when she finished her work in Saudi Arabia.

Amy was not sure how Beth would react if she told her about Pauline's experience, so decided not to tell her. It was some months before she eventually confessed what they had done. As she expected, Beth did not approve, but, as it was in the past, there was nothing to be done, other than to warn her of the foolishness of attempting to run before she could walk.

Shortly after Pauline returned to Saudi Arabia, Beth invited Amy to join her home circle, which would include novice mediums. Amy agreed to join, and she spent two years, along with Beth, helping them to develop.

One of the ways Amy helped her church was to transport speakers to and from the services. One of these was a medium named Edith, who lived near Amy. Edith had been a Spiritualist for over twenty five years, and held the CSNU in speaking and demonstrating. This is awarded by the Spiritualist National Union to speakers and demonstrators who reach a standard which they consider to be necessary for mediums working in churches affiliated to the union.

On one of the occasions when Amy took her home, Edith asked

her if she could add her name to her list of speakers and demonstrators who were available to fill in at short notice whenever a medium cancelled. She promised that she would also be on the rostrum, as chairperson, so if Amy felt she could not finish the service, she would help out. Amy agreed, little realising that she would receive a telephone call the following night, asking her to fill in for the Wednesday service.

Having Edith on the rostrum gave Amy confidence, and the service passed quickly. Amy could feel the energy coming from Edith, and found no difficulty in finishing the service herself. Amy was later to find that she would have to be careful who she shared a rostrum with, as some mediums, without realising what they are doing, drain energy from their co-workers. Edith, however, was like a spare battery, a source of energy, freely given, in case Amy felt the need of it.

Afterwards, Edith asked if she would like to take some bookings for more services in the church. Amy did not have a diary, other than the large desk diary which she used for her business, so Edith found a spare one, and gave it to her. Edith recommended Amy to other church secretaries, who were only too glad to have a medium that could fill in at the last moment. Edith also allowed Amy to share her evenings of clairvoyance at churches in the area. Amy did not realise that Edith was testing her, seeing if she was capable of taking over her bookings while she went into hospital for major surgery.

Taking over a busy medium's bookings took Amy away from her own church, other than the open circles, and there were raised eyebrows when she explained the reason for her absence. Because she was a new medium, and would be available at short notice, she was inundated with requests to 'fill in'. Amy hated to think of a church being let down, so never refused if she was free. At times she was doing three services a week. When she revealed this, she was told she was taking things too quickly and should slow down. Even one service a week was too much for a novice medium.

By now she knew enough to follow her instincts. She felt fine, and was not tired. She felt that she needed the 'shop floor' experience at that stage of her development, and there is an old saying that practice makes perfect. She was doing what Joseph had trained her to do and was not afraid, for she knew that she was never alone on the rostrum. All she had to do was reach out, and Mr. Latimer was there to help her.

There was someone else, too, someone she could not recognise. He stood directly behind her, while Mr. Latimer stood on her left. She knew that the man who stood behind her had great strength, and would always protect her if she needed it. Could this be her doorkeeper, the Native American whom she had previously thought to be her guide?

One night, during her meditation, she saw him again. He spoke to her. He told her to look in a book which she had on Native Americans, which would tell her about his tribe, the Comanche. The next day she found the book in her shop and took it home to read it when she had time. The following night, after her meditation, she read about the customs of the Comanche. It was extremely interesting, and not what is usually found in books. After she had finished she felt that she had had a lesson in the social, economic and spiritual ways of the Comanche.

A week later, she was talking to a customer who had asked for books on Native Americans. She told him about the book, and he said that he would be interested in buying it. She told him how informative it was, and said she would bring it to the shop for him to buy. Before she handed it over, she decided to read it again, to refresh her memory. She searched through the pages, looking for the chapter she had read. She could not find it, so thought she might be looking in the wrong book. However, this was the only book she had on that subject, so she scanned slowly through it again, with no success. In the end, she gave up, puzzled at her failure to find the chapter she had previously read and enjoyed.

Eventually she had to come to the conclusion that the information she had read was not in any book she possessed. Somehow, perhaps as a result of being overshadowed, or in a light trance, she had been shown what the Comanche doorkeeper wanted to her to see. She had also discovered her doorkeeper's name. It was Grey Wolf.

She was not able to verify the information she received, for there were no books on the Comanche available to her. She was also unable to explain why she could not provide her customer with the book she had promised him.

Now that she knew about Grey Wolf, she realised how he had influenced her throughout her life. This was probably where she had obtained her fascination with horses, for the Comanche were horse traders. When she owned horses, she realised that she had a knowledge which no-one had taught her. She knew instinctively what other people had learned from books. How could she tell why a horse was ill, or what would cure it? This had always mystified her. Especially what happened to Jupiter.

# Chapter Ten

There is a dedicated band of healers working in every Spiritualist church. This spiritual healing is recognised as a supportive aid to orthodox medicine. Sometimes spiritual healing is confused with faith healing. Those who question spirit intervention of any kind will state that any benefit derived from spiritual healing works on the principle that if the patient believes he will be cured, he will begin to feel better. If this was the case, then spiritual healing would not work on animals, for they know nothing about either spiritual or faith healing.

Working with animals for most of her adult life brought Amy into contact with their illnesses and injuries. She surprised herself (and the vet) on many occasions by diagnosing an illness which was not immediately apparent. The best example of this was when she called the vet to look at a pony mare belonging to one of her livery clients. He asked her what was wrong with the mare when she telephoned him, and she found herself saying that she thought the mare had an ovarian cyst. He laughed, but he was puzzled when he examined the mare internally and found she had a cyst the size of a golf ball on one of her ovaries. Amy was as surprised as the vet, because she could not explain how she had known the nature of the mare's illness.

Perhaps she had used her feminine intuition, recognising some of the mare's symptoms from gynaecological experiences of her own and those of her friends. That might be possible, except that Amy has never had an ovarian cyst, nor has she known anyone who has suffered from one. One of the mare's symptoms was that she was constantly 'horsing', that is, she was always in season. Amy had known promiscuous women in her lifetime, but none who blamed their behaviour on an ovarian cyst.

There was also a mare that was chronically lame. The vet diagnosed a shoulder injury, and prescribed pain killers. Amy protested that she believed the mare had broken her leg, but the vet explained how his diagnosis was correct, and Amy bowed to his professional opinion. Nevertheless, she was not happy. Something was telling her that the leg was broken, so she bandaged both of the mare's front legs to support them. There was no external abrasion, or noticeable swelling on the affected leg, but Amy had to follow her instincts that the leg was broken, and strapping it up was all she could do for the mare.

The next day, another vet came from the same practice and x-rayed the mare's leg. Once again, Amy said she thought the leg was broken, but the vet said that the x-ray would prove it one way or another. Later that morning he telephoned to say that there was no evidence of a break, but the leg was badly sprained. He asked if she knew how to 'blister' a horse. Amy said she did, and he asked if she would do it.

Amy was teaching girls on work experience at the time. They would not often get the opportunity to witness a horse being blistered, and she did not want to waste the chance of showing them how it was done.

Blistering involves clipping the hair from the leg, then applying a red paste, which burns the exposed skin, causing it to blister. The blood supply to the affected area is then increased, and both injuries heal more quickly. Amy hated doing it, because she considered it was barbaric. Nevertheless, it was a tried and tested old fashioned remedy which worked. However, the horse always experiences pain and irritation while the blistering takes effect. His instinct is to lick the affected part, so he has to be tied up on a very short rope so that he cannot reach his injury with his mouth.

They had just finished, and were discussing the pros and cons of blistering over a cup of coffee when the vet rang.

*"Have you blistered that mare yet?"* he asked.

Amy replied that she had, and he told her that he had studied the x-rays and found a hairline crack on the cannon bone. The leg was broken.

How had she known? Frankly, she could not explain it. Either she knew more about horses than she realised, or someone on the 'other side' was giving her the information. She experienced these same feelings every time a horse was sick or injured, and instinctively knew what to do to help them. Then, of course, there was Jupiter.

Jupiter was the first horse Amy bred. He was a 16.2 hands three quarter bred chestnut gelding out of her mare, Glory. He was still wet from his birth when Amy helped him to his feet, gave him his name, and promised him that he would be a racehorse one day. He was eight years old before she saved enough money to give him his chance, but he managed only one race before going lame. He was rested, and the following season, as he was being prepared for a race, he became lame again. This time, when he was examined, he was found to have a shoulder injury. It was a big disappointment, for he had been going particularly well, and had been entered in a race the following week.

Amy's eldest daughter, Teresa, had worked with race horses, and she accompanied her mother to the trainer's yard. Jupiter certainly looked as if he had injured his shoulder, and was putting his weight on the other side. Teresa removed his rugs, and they looked at him. His chestnut coat gleamed with well being, and he was a picture of good health except for his shoulder. It seemed a shame that he was going to miss the beginning of the season, and Amy felt that she had to do something to help him. What could she do that had not already been done?

*"Let me see if I can give him some spiritual healing,"* she said, and placed her hands on the affected shoulder.

She did not know what she was expected to feel, or what she thought would happen. There was no rush of heat to her hands and she did not experience a tingling sensation. Her hands were not directed to any particular spot, and she was disappointed, feeling that she could not do anything for the horse. Then she realised that she was the centre of attention, and began to feel foolish. Two pairs of eyes stared at her: one in horror, the other in amused disbelief. What was she doing, making herself into a laughing stock in front of her daughter and the trainer's wife?

*"Healing is obviously a very special gift, and I don't have it,"* she thought, wondering how to get out of the situation and still retain her dignity.

*"Do you think you've healed him?"* asked Anne, the trainer's wife. She was leaning over the bottom door of the stable, trying to keep a straight face. *"Will he be ready to race next week?"*

At that point in her development, sometimes words come out of Amy's mouth before she had a chance to think about them. She did not know what she was going to say until she heard herself speak. This was one such time.

*"The only thing I'm picking up from this horse is a headache."* she said.

As soon as the words were said, Amy felt silly. Teresa did not say anything, but her face was a picture as she put the rugs back onto the horse. She probably felt that her mother had finally flipped. It must have been difficult for Amy's daughters to have had a mother who was quite obviously away with the fairies.

*"I don't know about him having a headache,"* laughed Anne. *"He's been nothing but a headache to us since he got here. Are you coming into the house for a coffee?"*

They settled the horse and followed her into the house. Amy was glad that Anne did not mention her attempt at spiritual healing. Her idea of what was the natural and caring thing to do appeared eccentric to the others. She could see that Anne could hardly wait for them to go so she could tell her husband, Jim, what a crank they had for a client. Jim discussed Jupiter with Amy and they both decided to ask for a second opinion.

The following day the vet telephoned Amy to say that he had been to see Jupiter and had found the horse had dislocated the first vertebrae in his neck, just behind his ears. This had caused the lameness down one side, mimicking the symptoms of a shoulder injury. The vet had popped it back, and now Jupiter was much better. But he must have had a terrible headache!

Amy was annoyed when she heard the diagnosis. Why had she not had enough faith in herself to state that she felt that it was the head, not the shoulder which was causing pain? Because she had hesitated, the horse had suffered another day, and his training had been delayed.

Unfortunately, Jupiter did not become a star of the racing world. Spiritual healing helps, but it can't turn a goose into a swan or a slow horse into a Derby winner. He became lame again, and, because he was never likely to become a great racehorse, or even a good one, he returned home. All his venture into racing had done was to give him a bad leg and empty Amy's bank account.

It did not end there, however. It is virtually impossible to straighten a bowed tendon. The tendon is stretched, and never returns to normal. However, Amy was the original cock eyed optimist and never knew when she was faced with an impossible task. She smoothed his tendon every day, and when he left her, it was difficult to tell which leg had been affected. It may not have had anything to do with Amy, but it was the first time she had known a tendon become straight on its own. The horse did not know that she was giving him healing. In fact, I don't think that was Amy's intention. She merely touched his leg, as a mother would touch an injured child, saying, "Mummy will make it better." Jupiter did not realise, either, that he was receiving healing, so faith could have had nothing to do with it.

The art of horse whispering has become fashionable in recent years. Was that what Amy was doing? Is horse whispering a form of mediumship? This is something which would have to be studied in depth, and would be difficult to prove or disprove.

Perhaps, because she had an affinity with horses, she could commune with them in a way that all living beings communicated before language was introduced. Language separates people of different nationalities because they are unable to understand each other. Man relies too much on the spoken word, and does not tend to read body language the way he did in his early history.

Horses, and other animals, cannot speak as man does. In spite of this, they successfully communicate among themselves and with other species by signals comprising of sounds and body language. They respond to the body language of humans and instinctively know whether he is friend or foe.

Was Amy subconsciously interpreting Jupiter's body language when she felt that it was his head, and not his shoulder, he had injured? That could be possible, but how could she have possibly known that the mare had an ovarian cyst? That, I feel, was beyond the mare's comprehension, so we must conclude that Amy received the information in another way. Was it because she was mediumistic, or because she understood horses? Perhaps it was a combination of the two. Is that what horse whisperers do? I would think that horse whisperers are certainly sensitive, even psychic. Like Amy, they observe the horse and its behaviour. Through this they are able to sense the horse's needs and treat it accordingly. They communicate with the horse by body language and knowledge built upon their observations.

Spiritual healing is not meant to replace orthodox medicine. A healer is not supposed to diagnose, or suggest treatment. The patient always approaches the healer for treatment, not the other way around, and if the patient has not seen a doctor, the healer will always recommend he should consult one if it is necessary.

Spiritualist church services usually contain a minute of silent prayer for those who are sick in mind, body and spirit, followed by a healing hymn. Many Spiritualists, including Amy, compile a list of friends and acquaintances who may be in pain or are sick, and think of these during the healing silence, or during their personal prayers.

One day an elderly woman came into the bookshop. She was walking with difficulty and was obviously in pain. When Amy enquired what was wrong, the woman explained that her back was bad. Amy asked her name and said she would bring her into the healing circle the following night. She said this without thinking, for she automatically prayed for anyone in need of healing. The woman thanked her for her concern, and left the shop.

Amy thought no more about it, but included the woman in her own prayers as well as in the two services she attended. After the weekend, the woman came back to thank Amy for her prayers. Amy was not in the shop at the time, but the woman left her husband's name with the assistant, so that Amy could pray for him, too, as he also suffered with arthritis.

Amy wished she could have spoken to the woman, to explain that she was not a special person who had a direct line to God. Had the woman prayed herself she would have achieved the same result. She would have advised the woman to take her husband to the nearest Spiritualist church for healing, or, if he did not wish to go, to include his name in the absent healing book, so that thoughts and prayers could be sent out to him.

Amy found that prayer helped her. She prayed for people she knew needed healing, and received help in this way from others who were concerned whenever she was sick or in need of help. This restored her faith in her fellow man, knowing that some people really do care enough to pray for others.

Animals benefit from prayer too. Amy's old mare, Glory, became very ill. She refused to eat or drink and stood, her head almost touching the floor, as if waiting to die. Amy called the vet, but she had already prepared herself that she might lose the mare. Glory had come to Amy as a three year old, and was now seventeen. While she waited for the vet, Amy prayed that her lovely, gentle mare would get better. She also asked that, if Glory was going to die, it should be as quick and painless as possible. She rang Beth and asked her to pray for Glory. Beth telephoned people she knew, who in turn, telephoned other caring friends. Soon there was an army of Spiritualists and other caring people throughout the country praying for Glory.

When the vet examined the mare he shook his head. He warned Amy that the condition usually proved fatal between four and twenty four hours. He was very kind, and Amy knew that she could not have wished for more expert or concerned treatment for her mare. The vet called to see Glory twice a day, each time expecting to have to put her down.

Then suddenly, she began to improve. She began to pick at her hay, and was drinking her water. Soon she was her old self again, calling over the door of her box for her feed. The vet was surprised and almost as pleased as Amy. After a week he announced that he would not need to come back.

*"I can't believe that she's pulled through,"* he said, getting into his brand new Audi. *"I would have laid bets that she would not make it."*

Amy knew what he meant, for at the beginning of her illness, Glory had the appearance of a horse which had given up and was preparing to die. Horses do this. They can die from a bout of colic, which is basically stomach ache.

*"We've had a lot of help on our side,"* she pointed out. *"People all over the country have been praying for her."*

The vet was fastening his seatbelt as Amy said this. He'd known her for many years, and was used to her being different from other women, but this praying thing was definitely something new. If she had sworn at him, or told him a dirty joke, he would not have batted an eyelid. That was the Amy he knew. He looked her straight in the eyes, without a trace of a smile on his face.

*"I'm still going to send you my bill,"* he said, dryly, and drove off, scattering gravel as he sped down the drive to his next appointment.

As well as being good at his chosen profession, Amy felt that he might have a future as a straight man for a comedian.

In this modern world, when many illnesses are stress related, it can do no harm to slow down, perhaps say a prayer or meditate. It may even do a lot of good. At least, there will be no side effects, other than the positive feeling of well being.

At this time in her development Amy did not fully understand how the phenomenon of spiritual healing worked. She only knew that it did. She had witnessed the beneficial effects such healing could have on others, as well as on herself and her animals. It was not just the physical act of the laying on of hands. She knew that healing thoughts had the same results. Thoughts are living things, and have an effect on all our lives. Not only kind, positive and healing thoughts, for nasty, negative thoughts also shape the kind of person we are.

Her grandmother used to tell her, "Shy bairns get nowt." This has to be a true saying, for how can you expect anyone to come to your aid if you don't bring it to their attention that you need help? There is no shame in praying for yourself, or asking others to pray for you. You must have more chance of receiving help if you ask for it.

Amy has always worked on the principle that you do not knock anything until you have tried it. She has tried it, and found that it works. If it works for her, then it could work for you.

# Chapter Eleven

Amy's life was changing quickly. She needed to decide where her priorities lay and where she was going with Spiritualism. She was devoting more time to her work in the Spiritualist church and she had reached a point where she felt that perhaps she had accepted her mediumship too easily. Were the communications really from the world of spirit, or was she just merely sensitive, and able to pick information up from others, even read their minds? She needed to know that what she did brought comfort to those she tried to help, otherwise there was no point in continuing.

Why did she travel to churches within her area each Sunday to take services? She did not receive payment, other than money for petrol, so money could not be the driving force. Some mediums did private sittings or public demonstrations, for which they charged a fee, to supplement their income, but Amy was not one of them. It was not that she disapproved of mediums charging for sittings. She felt that it was not the road she wanted to go down. In her opinion, mediums who did this served people who would not otherwise receive the help they needed. There are many who think that, unless they pay for something, it is worthless. Amy regularly saw members of the congregation sort out a five pence piece to put in the collection after a good service in a church, then gladly pay ten or fifteen pounds for a private sitting.

There are also those who would not, for various reasons, wish to be seen in a Spiritualist church, but at the same time, feel that visiting a psychic would be quite fashionable.

In order to stand in front of a congregation week after week, a medium needs to have decent clothes. Not all mediums can afford these. So how do they manage? Some, like Amy, trawl the charity shops for bargains. Others use money they earn from sittings to provide them with a good wardrobe and a decent car, two necessary pieces of equipment for their spiritual work within the churches.

Amy, like most mediums, cannot remember most of the evidence she gives from the platform. She is not meant to, for she is just the messenger. However, now and then, one message sticks in her mind, and this is usually the evidence that she has needed to prove to her that she is doing a worthwhile job.

One such occasion happened when she was still in the development class. As she sat in the open circle, she felt as if she was being hemmed in, yet was afraid to go out. She was uncomfortable, and looked around the circle until she saw the person she felt was suffering that condition. It was a long time before she got up, because there were a lot of mediums working that night, but it was a relief when she was able to do so.

Instead of asking the woman if she could speak to her, Amy was inspired to take the woman's hands, which she did.

*"I've come to help you,"* she said.

The look on the woman's face told Amy that she was relieved that someone knew she needed help.

*"I feel as if I am in a tiny room,"* continued Amy. *"My life means nothing. There is nothing for me outside this room, and my whole life is centred on it. Life has no meaning. I only exist from one day to the next."*

The woman nodded, and said that was the way she felt. Amy continued to relay messages to the woman from her father, who was in spirit. The woman seemed pleased, and it was obvious by her reaction that she had been very close to her father.

After the circle, one of the younger women who had accompanied the woman to the church approached Amy.

*"Excuse me,"* she said, shyly. *"Would you come and have a word with my mother, please?"*

Amy went over to the family and spoke to the woman. Then she realised that they were sitting very close to the woman, acting as a protective screen.

*"I suffer from agoraphobia,"* the woman announced. *"I haven't been out of the house for years. It took all of these,"* (she indicated her family,) *to get me here tonight. The way you described my condition is exactly the way I feel."*

Amy talked to the woman, and as she left her, she said she would see her the following week in church. She was delighted when she arrived at the church the following week to find the woman and her family sitting in the circle.

Among the regulars at the church were a couple named Ann and Bill. Amy had not spoken to them, other than to say good evening, but she will always remember the effect she had on Bill the first time he came to the open circle. His face showed that he was apprehensive, and a little afraid of what was about to happen. He sat, wide eyed, not daring to move in case he drew attention to himself. He wore a large gold crucifix around his neck, which he fingered now and then, perhaps to reassure himself that he was protected against harm. Every time Amy sneaked a look at him, her mind was filled with information to give him.

As soon as she was able, she approached him.

*"May I speak with you?"* she asked.

Bill nodded, his eyes growing wide with apprehension as he clutched his crucifix. Amy then related to him the information she had in her mind and he accepted it, stunned at how accurate and detailed it was.

After that, Ann and Bill were regular visitors to the open circle, as well as the Sunday night service. They were a popular couple, and friendly with everyone. Bill could not get enough of this wonderful phenomenon, and he was a medium's delight, because he was so open and friendly.

A few months later, Ann came to the open circle on her own, because Bill was recovering from influenza, and did not feel up to going out. After the circle, she talked to Amy, discussing the evening's events. Amy felt she had to put her hands either side of Ann's face, cupping it.

*"When you go home,"* she said. *"Do this to Bill, but don't tell him who told you to do it."*

Ann laughed, and went home, carrying members' good wishes for Bill's recovery. The following week she again came to the circle alone. After the service she took Amy to one side. She explained that when she had returned home the previous week she had found Bill in a distressed state. After she had left for church, he had received a telephone call to tell him that his elder sister, who had acted as a mother to him, had died in hospital following a heart attack. Knowing how close he was to his sister, Ann tried her best to comfort him. Then she remembered what Amy had told her to do.

*"I was told at the church to do this,"* she said, cupping his face in her hands.

He became very emotional, and asked who had told her to do it. She replied that she had been specifically told not to tell him. He then explained that, when he was a boy, whenever he became upset, his sister would cup his face in her hands to comfort him. Ann got shivers down her spine when he told her this, and confessed that Amy had told her to do it.

It was not clear to Amy when she sent the message to Bill why she should want to cup his face in her hands. She had merely felt impressed to do it. As she passed over, Bill's sister had reached out to him. In her concern and love for her younger brother, she had found the only way she could to relay this to him. Amy was merely the tool available at the time.

This episode answered Amy's doubts. It was an acceptable reason why she should continue working for the Spiritualist movement. Soon after that, she joined the Spiritualists National Union, where a whole new world opened for her. She had not realised that the

Union provided education courses, and once she started to learn, most of her questions were answered.

It was about this time that Amy was impressed to write. Although she had always wanted to write, she had found it difficult, for she could not type. Anyone who has tried to write a novel in longhand will understand how she became discouraged. At the time, she did not realise that, if you are meant to do something which aids the work you do for the movement, whatever you need to complete the task will be provided.

When a man came to her shop to sell books, then offered her a second hand electric typewriter, she jumped at it. If she was serious about writing she would have to learn to type. She did not try it out until she got home, so it was a relief to find that it worked perfectly.

Teresa showed her how to put a margin in, and what all the keys were for. Amy was impatient to start, but when she did, she made so many mistakes that she had to give it up as a bad job. Teresa tried her best, but it was no use. Amy just could not type. She was very disappointed, for she had an idea for a novel, which she wanted to get down onto paper.

The typewriter sat on the dining table, gathering dust. Carolyn promised to help Amy when she was on holiday, but that was months away. Amy felt so frustrated. The novel was building up in her head, the plot was becoming more intricate, and she had begun to feel that the characters were real people.

Then one night, after everyone had gone to bed, she inserted a piece of paper into the typewriter and began to type. Slowly but surely the manuscript grew and by the time she went to bed she felt that she had achieved something. She was not very fast, but the spacing was more or less correct, and although there were some mistakes, it was a very passable effort.

She began to write every night. Not the novel, as she had planned, but stories of her experiences. Slowly but surely, the manuscript grew, and by the time she went to bed she always felt that she had achieved something. She began to make fewer mistakes, and became quicker. She was thoroughly enjoying herself, and she never had to stop to think what she should write next. She felt Mr. Latimer beside her as she wrote, and she knew that it was him who had given her the discipline to finish what she had started. By the end of the week she had written twenty four thousand words. Some feat for a total beginner! How had she managed to do this? As she looked back over the manuscript, she could see where Mr. Latimer had impressed his thoughts on hers and she knew that she had not been alone.

Carolyn took the manuscript away and typed it professionally, with double spacing and the correct margins. She made two copies and bound both of them. Amy was so pleased when she saw her book, although at twenty four thousand words, it hardly merited the title. However, it had the makings of one. Once the flesh was added to its bones it would be two or three times the size.

She consulted the Writers and Artists Year Book and found an agent who she thought might be interested in her work. Trying to sound businesslike, she typed a covering letter and sent it off, with a stamped addressed envelope for its return. Two days later, it arrived back. She was devastated. He did not like it! She was not a writer!

Then she opened the envelope. Inside was a very encouraging letter from the agent, saying that, although her work was well written, it would not be a commercial proposition. He added that he would like to see any fiction which she was working on.

From being in the depths of despair, she was walking on air. He liked the way she wrote! A proper London agent wanted to see her novel!

The next few weeks saw Amy hard at work until the early hours of the morning, writing the first three chapters of her novel, a family saga. The plot buzzed in her head, and as she wrote, she added to it: subconsciously weaving a pattern without realising that she was laying the ground for happenings later in the book. The words flowed onto the page, her fingers struggling to keep up with her thoughts.

The following two weeks were almost unbearable as she waited for the agent to reply. Each day she walked to the mail box with mixed feelings: hoping to hear from him, yet afraid of another rejection. Then a letter, not the manuscript, arrived. He liked it, and wanted to see the rest of it! He also sent notes on successful saga writing, explaining what readers preferred.

There was no holding Amy now. She was a writer, a proper one, with an agent! Page after page, she glided through the story, enjoying every minute of it. Her characters laughed; cried; loved; died. She began to dislike a couple of them, and even fancied one of them. Even if it was never published, she knew it had to be finished: this story had to be told.

The finished manuscript was more than a hundred and eighty thousand words and cost five pounds to post. It had taken five months to produce. As a precaution, she enclosed a stamped addressed envelope for its return, in case the agent did not like it. There was no need, for the manuscript did not come back. Instead, she opened another letter from the agent which began 'Congratulations on having written a really good saga. I am most impressed.' The agent then went on to say that, in its present state, it was not ready for publication, and would have to be edited. He explained that in parts Amy had been a little long winded, and enclosed a few sample pages which he had edited to show her how to improve her work. He ended by saying that he had no doubt that she would be successfully published.

She could hardly believe that she had succeeded with her first effort. She wanted to get straight to work on the second draft of her book, so that she could see her work in print. She was half way through it when the bottom fell out of her world.

It was the beginning of May, and Geoff was driving her to the shop. They were stationary at a roundabout, waiting for an opening in the traffic. Geoff was a good driver who knew the capabilities of his vehicle. A Volvo estate, fully loaded, needs a decent space to enter the flow of traffic safely. Amy had her eyes closed, and was thinking of a twist to improve the ending of her book. There was a loud bang, as if the car was falling apart, and she was thrown forward. The seat belt restrained her, but her head whipped back and struck the head rest.

She was groggy when she got out of the car, and sat on the grass verge for a while, trying to clear her head. Black treble clefs floated in front of her eyes and as she looked around she realised that the car had been rammed by a speeding taxi driver who had thought they were about to pull away. The front of the taxi was badly damaged, which was not surprising. Hitting a stationary Volvo estate which had the hand brake on, at speed, must have been like hitting a stone wall.

At the hospital, she was diagnosed to have a whiplash injury, with no broken bones. She was initially relieved, but she had not realised how much it would affect her writing. She could not sit for any length of time at the typewriter, or bend her neck. Her head ached constantly, and she generally felt unwell. She was told that this would clear up with a matter of months, but it continued to restrict her activities, especially her writing, for many years.

Being unable to type did not mean that she was not working on her novel. Occasionally, she took the manuscript and a thick pencil, and made an attempt to edit it. She could only do this for a short time and soon became dispirited. To make matters worse, she was swamped with bookings for services. There was a shortage of mediums at that time, especially during holiday periods, and Amy did not know how to say no to a church secretary in need.

The most frustrating part of her injury was not being able to be 'hands on' with her horses. Seeing others doing her work made her feel useless and lazy. There were so many calls on her time, that she felt she was not doing anything well, and she became depressed. It was about this time that Susan began to get unwelcome spirit visitors at night, and Amy had to forget her own problems in order to help her daughter. She turned to Beth for help, and it was she who introduced Amy to astral travel.

# Chapter Twelve

The moment she heard Susan's voice, Amy knew she was in trouble. All the fears a woman has when her daughter lives away from home flooded through her mind. She was relieved when she found out that the problems were not physical. Susan was a sensible girl, and could cope with most of what life threw at her. So it was no wonder that Amy was worried, when her sensible capable daughter, who had never needed help before, called, especially when she asked if her father was in the room. She did not want him to know that she was having problems, particularly as it was her who had lectured Amy on the dangers of 'dabbling' with Spiritualism. Perhaps she thought that it was her mother's involvement in Spiritualism which was causing her to receive uninvited spirit visitors in the night. Amy tried to help her as far as her knowledge allowed. She told her to acknowledge the spirit, and to ask him/her to go away.

Susan explained that she was being woken during the night by a heavy weight on her chest, which made it difficult for her to breathe. Amy had heard of others experiencing this, and how terrified they had felt, being pinned to the bed by an unseen force. She tried to reassure Susan, but she knew what her daughter was going through. Hadn't she felt the same, when the presence first came to her bedside? She promised to ask her friends for help, and when Susan put the phone down, Amy immediately dialled another number.

Beth listened as Amy described Susan's experience, now and then interrupting, to clarify a point. When Amy had finished, Beth said that she had done the right thing, and hopefully, the spirit would do as Susan asked, and go away.

*"If she has any more trouble, I'll visit her."* she said.

*"She lives over thirty miles away, but I'll drive you there,"* said Amy, knowing that Beth did not drive.

*"I wasn't meaning to go by car."* laughed Beth.

It was a moment or two before Amy understood what she meant. She knew that Beth frequently 'visited' friends and relatives who were ill, to give them healing, or to help them in other ways, without leaving her own home. She was talking about soul projection, sometimes confused with astral travel.

Amy had learned the definition of astral travel in the development class. She knew it was travel by the spirit (or soul), independently of the body. This usually happened when the body was asleep, or the traveller was in deep meditation. She had never consciously experienced this phenomenon herself: there were times when she thought she might have been travelling, but had put the experience down to dreams.

Susan lived in lodgings on the outskirts of a small village. Her job, stable lass in a large racing yard, was arduous and not very well paid, so she supplemented her income by working behind the bar in one of the village's two pubs. It was safe to assume that her experiences were not induced by boredom, or an over active imagination. By the time she reached her bedroom at night, she was exhausted, and had no trouble in getting to sleep.

Amy wondered if she had been right to advise Susan to send the spirit away. What if he/she was her guide, or a family member, wanting to be near? Was she right to deny Susan the opportunity to meet these spirit helpers, to enjoy the experiences she herself had had? Then again, Susan was thirty years younger than her mother, and she did not have the time to become involved with Spiritualism, even if she had wanted to. What was right for Amy, at her time of life, might not be right for her daughter.

All was well for a couple of days, then Susan telephoned again. She had done what Amy had said, and it had worked for two nights, but not the third. Amy promised her daughter that she would get her some help, and rang Beth once again. Beth asked her to establish what time Susan normally went to sleep, and where her bedroom was in relation to the bathroom and the top of the stairs. Amy did this, reassuring Susan that help really was on the way, and that she would soon go back to having uninterrupted sleep. Then Beth dropped the bombshell.

*"You're coming with me,"* she said.

*"But I've never done anything like this before, and I don't know if I can do it,"* protested Amy, her heart racing her reason, and winning by a short head.

*"You'll be with me, and Mr. Latimer will also be there,"* replied Beth. *"He will not allow you to go if you aren't ready for it. Have some faith in yourself and your guide. Mr. Latimer will make sure that you come to no harm."*

Amy still was not happy about this new experience, but Susan needed her help, and she could not let her down. When your children are in trouble, you often do things you would not normally do in order to help them. Amy knew how she felt when she had first experienced an uninvited nocturnal visitor, and she recognised that Susan must have been desperate to even admit that she was being troubled by spirits.

The plan was that Beth and Amy would both meditate at eleven o' clock that night. Luckily, Geoff went to bed early, so he was safely out of the way. Amy had to make sure that the dogs were settled. She did not know what to expect, but she knew that it would not help matters if one of the dogs jumped onto her lap in the middle of whatever they were about to do.

Everything was ready. She took one last look around the room, then sat in Geoff's chair. She looked at the clock. It was exactly eleven. Her heart thumping, she tried to relax and clear her mind. Normally, when she meditated, she closed her eyes, relaxed, then a few minutes later would be aware of Mr. Latimer on her left side, then Grey Wolf would stand behind her. Usually, the first thing she saw was a thick, swirling mist. Sometimes it would remain grey, but more often it turned to a dusky pink, which in turn deepened to a lilac, then purple. If she was lucky, she would see images in her mind's eye. This time, however, there was no hanging about. Grey Wolf and Mr. Latimer were both in their places, ready to be off. She felt as if she was late for class and they could not start without her. Perhaps she should have allowed some time for preparations before the rendezvous at eleven.

She did not feel she was walking: it was more like being propelled forwards through a thick, mushroom coloured swirling mist. She felt as if she was standing on a platform or trolley which was moving forward. She was on her way.

It never occurred to her, or worried her, that she could not see Beth. Her mind no longer functioned in its usual way, and instructions she was not aware of receiving were being fed directly into her thoughts. At the same time, she was well aware of her experience, and what was going on around her.

Then someone appeared out of the mist, arms outstretched in greeting. Amy knew that this was a spirit, but had no feelings towards him at all. Nor was she afraid. She accepted that spirits would be there, so was not surprised when they appeared. It was as if they were passers by in a street who wanted to stop and chat with her, but she did not want to find out their identities. She was there to do a specific job, and stopping to speak to passers by was not part of it. She had to get on, and remain focussed. Waving the spirit to one side, she continued on her journey.

*"I'm sorry. I can't stop. I've got a job to do,"* she heard herself repeating as she brushed more and more spirits aside. They were all pleased to see her, and wanted to greet her, but Amy knew that she had to say and do what she was being instructed by her guide.

They still came forward, smiles on their faces, wanting her to recognise them, and to spend a short time with her. She could not put a name to any of them, because she knew she was not supposed to recognise them. If she did, she might be tempted to stay with them, and not achieve what she had gone into the spirit world to do. Still she could not see Beth, but she was not worried. Her companions knew where to go and what to do.

Onwards through the mist she went, marvelling at the pure, subtle pastel colours until she finally came to stop in an area where the mist was not so thick, a sort of a clearing. Here the mist did not swirl around, but hung in wisps here and there.

A man stood a short distance away, dressed in a dark pinstriped suit. His thinning brown hair was swept back off his face and he looked old fashioned, probably dating to the post world war two era. He turned towards her, then turned profile and bent from the waist, like a butler making an exaggerated bow. Although Amy did not recognise him, she knew he was her father. As soon as she thought this, things changed. Her task was completed: she was only there to identify the spirit and now that she had, there was no reason for her to stay any longer. Then she heard a voice, which she recognised as her own.

*"I'm sorry, Beth. I'll have to go back."*

No sooner had she said this than she felt herself moving backwards. The return journey was much faster than the outward one and she saw no spirit people. She seemed to land in the chair with a thump. She opened her eyes and looked at the clock. It was twenty five past eleven! It did not seem possible that she had been away so long, and she was so surprised that she forgot to thank Mr. Latimer and Grey Wolf for taking her into the spirit world.

She had not told Susan that Beth would be 'visiting' her, or in what manner. It was better that she did not know what they were doing. Amy was not sure that Susan would have believed her, and also, if she did not know, she could not be influenced, and they would get a true reaction from her. A couple of days later, she rang and said that she had had no more trouble.

Beth and Amy decided that they should introduce Susan to a Spiritualist church near her digs, so that she could obtain help locally if she needed it. There were two churches nearby, and they chose one because it had an open circle on Wednesdays, which meant that they could accompany her. They arranged to meet her at her lodgings the following Wednesday.

Anyone who has been to this particular SNU church will know how welcome they were made to feel. The people were friendly, and put Susan at her ease, which was no mean feat. Her convent education had instilled in her a deep rooted prejudice against Spiritualism. She had been taught that it was akin to worshipping the devil, and had not previously wanted to be drawn into anything which would prevent her immortal soul from reaching Heaven.

Despite their efforts, and the warm welcome she had received in the church, Susan did not return there for help. Amy was disappointed, for she knew there were people within that church who were both able and willing to help Susan. You can take a horse to water........! However, Susan reported no more problems for many months. She also changed her job and went to work for a horse dealer. This gave her the opportunity to ride in point to points, which are amateur steeplechases. She stayed at this job for a couple of seasons then moved to another racing stable, three hundred miles away from home.

She was happy in her new job. She was treated by the trainer as one of the family, but she had to move after a few months. The stable was having financial difficulties, so the trainer had to let her go. Because of this, she had to get another job quickly, especially as it was only a few weeks before Christmas. Amy tried to get her to come home for Christmas, and to have a week or so holiday before taking another job, but Susan had little money, and wanted to get a job immediately, which she did.

After a few months in her new job, Susan began to experience more psychic phenomena, and could not sleep through the night without being woken by spirits. Even during the day, on her way to or from a race meeting, as she dozed in the horse box, she found herself being roused by spirit voices.

When she came home for a holiday, she confessed that this was happening, and she did not sleep any better at home. Amy talked the problem through with her, explaining that Susan had to take control of this situation herself. She had to explain to the spirit friends who bothered her that she knew they were there, but needed to sleep. It had to be a case of 'don't call me. I'll call you when I want to talk to you.' Her job was physically demanding and the trainer was not the ideal employer. He was eccentric, and this put a strain on his employees.

Amy explained to Susan about energy centres, which are situated in various parts of the body. These can be closed or opened, and Susan needed to know how to 'close up', so that she was not receptive to spirit communications until she felt that she wanted to communicate with spirits. As long as they remained open, she was likely to be aware of spirits. Amy gave her a leaflet, with a diagram of the energy centres and information about them, so she could refer to it whenever she wished.

As Amy thought through her daughter's problems, she realised that Susan only had her 'visitors' when she was unsettled, or unhappy. Perhaps she was subconsciously reaching out for help, and when it came, was afraid of the helper. There was no doubt that Susan was psychic, and perhaps one day she would follow Amy into the Spiritualist church, but for the moment, she wanted to get on with her material life.

It was Susan's choice to ask her spirit friends to go, and she had a right to do it. We are all personally responsible for what we say and do, so it follows that we should have the privilege of choosing our own path in life. Amy did not want to influence Susan in any way. If she chose Spiritualism, then Amy would give her all the help she needed, but if she did not, that was fine, too. You do not need to be a Spiritualist to lead a spiritual life: you need to be spiritual, which Amy knew that Susan was.

What happened to Susan is a common occurrence. Unfortunately, not many realise that what they are experiencing will not hurt them. Their fear, fuelled by superstition, religious beliefs, supernatural fiction, or any combination of the three, is the cause of their grief. There is nothing supernatural about the spirit world. It is part of nature. After physical death, the soul continues to exist in another dimension, and is capable of communicating with those souls who still inhabit a physical body.

We can't all spare the time, or have the inclination to communicate with etheric beings. We could say that those who are in spirit have had their physical lives, so why don't they leave us in peace to get on with ours? They will, as long as we do not encourage, or invite them to speak to us. As long as they see an open door, they presume they are welcome. Learn to close the door and you will learn control. Then you can open the door whenever it suits you.

After their success with Susan, Beth suggested that they should 'visit' a mutual friend, who was ill in hospital. She was most surprised when Amy refused.

*"Why not?"* She asked. *"You've done it before. You know what it's like now."*

*"Precisely,"* replied Amy. *"It's because I've tried it that I'll never do it again."*

*"But everything went well. You came to no harm."* Beth pointed out. *"And you'd be helping a friend."*

*"I'll send my thoughts out to her,"* replied Amy. *"But I'll never do that again as long as I live."*

*"Never is a long time,"* smiled Beth. *" Things change. There will be a time when you change, too. You should never say 'never'."*

*"All right, then,"* laughed Amy. *"At this moment in my life, I do not ever want to try astral travel again. I only did it because Susan needed me. I don't think I'd be able to do it for anyone other than my own close family."*

Her reaction puzzled Beth, for she had expected Amy to have wanted to continue with this new phenomenon. During her development, Amy had always been the one who was eager to try something new: always the first to volunteer. She had been keen to learn and had never appeared to know the meaning of the words caution or fear. She did not attempt to change Amy's mind. That was not her style, but she was curious to know the reason why Amy shied away from repeating her experience.

Amy could not tell her, because she did not know herself. She always used her feelings as a yardstick: if she felt she was being pushed to do something, she did it, because it seemed right. She had not got that feeling with her experience of astral travel. She was not exactly glad it was over, but she had no ambition to try it again. Until she fully understood what she had done, she would not be happy. Had she really gone into the spirit world? Or, having had it suggested to her, had she imagined, or even dreamed it? Why could she do it that night, and not other times when she had 'linked in' with Beth to meditate? Had she done it herself, or had Beth done it for her? Amy did not relish the idea of being a passenger. She had to be in control in whatever she did. Guidance was one thing, but this was a different ball game.

She also felt that, although she herself had gone into the spirit world, Beth had not. What she had done was to project her soul, or spirit to Susan in order to administer the help she needed. Amy did not know that she would like to do this, however noble the reason. It felt to her that she would be invading someone's privacy.

There was the possibility that, under Beth's teaching, she had progressed further, and the way was open to repeat her experience. Could she manage to do it without Beth's assistance? Amy did not feel an overpowering desire to find out, so felt that perhaps it was better to wait until she did. At that moment in time, there was not a good enough reason to attempt it again. So, for the foreseeable future, she felt she should be prudent. Until she felt differently, she would regard astral travel and soul projection as something she knew was possible, but was something which other people did.

It would seem at this point that Geoff was the only 'normal' person in the family. He was a down to earth, easy going, hard working man, fiercely protective towards his family and home. He was also probably the most sceptical person anyone could hope to meet. Despite the many examples of psychic phenomena that Amy experienced, he maintained that there was always a logical explanation for them. However, things happened to him, too, although he refused to attribute them to the work of spirit helpers.

One day, Amy returned home to find him pacing the floor. He was visibly upset, and could not settle down.

*"I've had a feeling all morning that my brother, Bill, is dead,"* he said. *"And that bloody wife of his has buried him without telling me."*

Bill and Doreen were one of the closest, most loving couples

Amy knew. They lived three hundred miles away, and got in touch only at Christmas and family celebrations. Amy could not believe that Doreen would have done such a thing, and said so.

*"Ring Doreen,"* she said. *"Put your mind at rest."*

*"I wouldn't give her the satisfaction,"* he snarled.

Amy was shocked at the emotion behind his words. He was angry and upset, and really believed that Bill was dead. However much she tried, she could not persuade him to telephone his brother. She did not want to interfere, so left it at that. The following day, Amy answered the telephone to Bill's youngest daughter, who asked to speak to her uncle Geoff.

*"How is your dad?"* asked Amy

*"Why do you ask?"* she replied then went on. *"My dad had an operation for a hernia yesterday morning. He 'died' on the operating table, and was 'dead' for three minutes, but they revived him, and he's O.K. now."*

Amy handed the telephone to Geoff, and he heard the full story. He was stunned when he put the phone down. For once he could not think of a logical explanation. How had he known that Bill had 'died'? He'd had no communication with Bill or his family for months, and had no idea that he was to have this operation.

There have been many documented cases of near death experiences, where people have described entering a spirit world, or looking down on themselves as surgeons struggled to revive them. Sceptics say that these experiences are hallucinations, brought on by chemical changes in the brain. However, Geoff also experienced his brother's 'demise'. He was fully fit, and certainly was not hallucinating, or on mind altering drugs. So how did he know?

Could it be that Bill's spirit, at the moment of 'death', left his body, and attempted to say goodbye to his only brother? No? Then what could it have been? Sceptics may say it was telepathy. Perhaps they are right. Telepathy is the transferring of thoughts from one mind to another. Spirits communicate by thought transference, and man is spirit within a physical body. I rest my case.

# Chapter Thirteen

Things settled down with Susan, leaving Amy to concentrate on her writing and her church work. The second draft of her novel was coming along very slowly because of the pain it caused her to sit at the typewriter. Sometimes she did not go near it for months. The accident had not only caused physical injuries, it had taken away the motivation to write. She did not have writer's block, or lack inspiration, for the plot of the novel was constantly in her head. She had begun to think of the sequel and even a third book to make up a trilogy, but shied away from sitting at the typewriter because of the pain it caused her.

She was also experiencing problems with her left shoulder which were attributed to the accident. The pain increased and the mobility in the shoulder got less, so it was inevitable that she would have to undergo surgery. Amy has had two operations on her left shoulder, but still has problems with it and it still continues to affect her writing.

This was frustrating, for the more she thought about the plot, the more involved she became with the characters. She felt that she knew them personally, and wanted desperately to get their story down on paper. Yet each time she began to type, all she could think of was how much it hurt her to sit there. This depressed her, and she felt that things could not possibly get any worse. But they could. And they did!

The local water company moved onto the land next to her home and began to construct a sewage pipe which ran out to the sea. There were also plans to build a sewage treatment plant, just yards from her home. One by one her livery customers left, taking their horses to a safer place. The stables shared a common entrance from the main road with the water company, and customers had to pass the construction site to get to and from the stables. The first thing the company did was to widen the access road to accommodate their heavy wagons, and while they did this it became dangerous to ride horses on it. There were also a couple of near misses, where ponies, frightened by the noise and fluttering fluorescent tape, bolted onto the main road. Some of these ponies had been with Amy for up to ten years, and were what is known as 'bombproof', but they could not always cope with the noise of large trucks combined with the sudden movement of the tape as the wind blew it across their path. The safety of their young riders had to be her prime concern, and she worried because this could not be guaranteed. Within weeks all of her livery clients had moved elsewhere. This made it difficult for Amy to afford to keep her own horses, and she had to face the possibility that they would have to go.

They had the smallholding on an agricultural tenancy, so whatever effect the sewage treatment plant would have on the value of their home would not affect them financially, other than the loss of income from the livery clients. At the same time, they had sunk all of their capital into the property during the fifteen years they had lived there, and were not in a good position to find another place to live.

Their landlord contacted them and offered a fair settlement to move because he wanted to sell the property to the water company. Had Amy been in better health, and able to look after her horses herself, she might have refused to move until the landlord could come up with alternative accommodation for her family and her animals. However, she had to admit that her riding days were probably over, and a sum of compensation which was agreeable to both sides was reached. Geoff and Amy found themselves with thirteen weeks in which to find and purchase another home. They also had to find homes for Amy's horses.

During this hectic and stressful time, Amy never cancelled any of her church work. She found the church therapeutic: a calming pool to plunge into, a sanctuary from the chaos that her life had become.

That summer was very wet and they dripped their way through many houses without finding the right one. Moving house is always a stressful experience, but this was combined with finding homes for her beloved horses, too. Conscious that they had a deadline to meet, they thought they would never manage to find a house that suited their needs before their time ran out. Then one Saturday, after looking through the property section in the local paper, Amy walked into their shop.

*"I'm going to walk around the streets,"* she said. *"I'll go to places I'd like to live then walk around looking at 'for sale' boards."*

They had already viewed a house in the same village as the church. It faced onto open farmland and had only pedestrian access to the front of the property. The house was very nice, but was not quite what they wanted. It only had two bedrooms, which did not allow for both daughters to visit at the same time. There were two other sale boards displayed in that street, and Amy picked her way along the overgrown footpath at the front of the terraced houses, hoping to see her dream home. Then she saw the sorriest looking house she had ever seen in her life.

The front garden fence had been knocked down and children had obviously been using the garden as an adventure playground. A cherry tree had taken advantage of the lack of human attention and put out suckers all over the lawn, some of which were five or six feet high. Amy peered across this jungle to the boarded up bay windows, and the house seemed to reach out to her. Excited, she made her way to the back of the house and peered through the door into the back yard.

The back of the house looked worse than the front. The concrete in the yard was crazed with deep cracks, in which huge purple weeds grew. Still, Amy felt that this was her house, and she took the estate agent's number.

*"I've found our house!"* she cried, triumphantly waving the paper with the agent's number on.

Then the hard part began. There was much to do in the house.

It had been empty for over two years and had been vandalised. It had also been occupied for a while by squatters. There was so much to do, both inside and out, and Amy was hampered by the fact that only Susan shared her enthusiasm for the house. Nobody else could see beyond the work that needed to be done. The newspapers had reported that it was a house buyer's market and there were many bargains to be had, but that was not the case with this house. It took a lot of haggling, heart searching and argument, before they bought it and moved in.

Glory's last foal, Vulcan, was four years old and was an exceptionally good looking horse. Amy had planned to stand this horse as a stallion, but now he would have to be sold. Because a four year old colt would prove hard to sell, he was gelded. He was very sick afterwards, and it took a lot of dedicated nursing to pull him round. He went to the very best possible home and Amy was happy for him. Glory and her granddaughter, Juno, were farmed out for the summer until Amy could get herself sorted out. It was a great wrench to have to part with horses which had been part of the family for so long. Only Glory had been bought in, but she had been with Amy for sixteen years. She had bred the others, planned their conception, attended to their birth, and named them.

Five Jack Russell terriers made up the rest of the family. Two of these did not get on with the other three, and had been kept apart on the smallholding. That was one of the reasons that the new house was so perfect. Harry and Lucy could live in the back of the house, while Tim, his daughter, Dolly and granddaughter, Meg, lived in the front.

It may seem strange that Amy should choose a house to suit the dogs, but she felt that she had an obligation to make sure they were as happy and comfortable as possible. Tim was now thirteen and a half and had congestive heart disease. The others, all related to him, were getting on in years, too. At six, Harry was the youngest. They had all served the family well as vermin controllers. They had also been good companions, so Amy felt it was only right that they should be allowed to live the rest of their lives in honourable retirement.

The dogs adapted quickly to their new life, except Meg, who curled up on Geoff's chair, shivering, with half closed eyes, waiting to be taken home. The dogs were not used to having neighbours, so they barked every time they heard someone in the back lane or on the footpath at the front of the house. This path was used frequently by dog owners and the proximity of other dogs to their home enraged the terriers.

Unfortunately, neighbours do no appreciate noisy dogs, especially when they come in a pack of five. Amy was apologetic and tried to explain that the dogs would eventually become used to their new home and consequently accept passers by. This did not prevent someone from sending them an anonymous letter, or reporting them to the local council. Tim's eyesight was beginning to fail, and Amy was pleased that he was now confined to a smaller area.

Teresa was expecting a baby, and stayed with her parents most weekends. She lived in a town ten miles away, and was having problems with some of her neighbours, so was glad of the peace she found in the new house. As her pregnancy progressed, she began to stay longer, only going home occasionally, to check the house and to pick up her mail.

The baby was due in November, and, according to the scan, was a boy. Teresa began to ask questions about Amy's father, which Amy answered to the best of her knowledge. Teresa decided to call the baby Daniel William. William was Amy's father's name, and Daniel was a name which Teresa had chosen herself.

Amy's father's birthday was on the twenty first of October, and on the eighteenth, three weeks before Daniel was due, Amy went to church. It was a rare treat to sit in the congregation and enjoy a service, especially with such a good speaker.

The speaker was a very experienced, spiritual medium, and Amy always found her services both uplifting and inspiring. On that Sunday night the philosophy was really good, but when she began her demonstration, the medium hesitated.

*"I don't usually work like this,"* she began. *"But I have a gentleman here, who is saying that it is his birthday today. Can anyone take*

*this?"*

Nobody answered. Amy nearly put her hand up, because her father's birthday was so close, but while she was thinking about it, a woman said that she knew someone who's birthday it was the following day. The medium gave the woman the message. Amy realised that it had been her message, because she could understand everything the medium said. The woman was not sure, so the medium said she would have to leave her, as the link was weak. Her eyes swept the congregation then rested on Amy.

*"May I speak with you?"* she asked.

Amy answered 'yes'. The medium began to talk about Amy's grandmother, her father, and other things which Amy knew she had no knowledge of. Then she dropped a bombshell.

"That man's back again. He is insisting that it is his birthday today, and he's singing 'Danny Boy.' Would that mean anything to you?"

Amy accepted the message, thinking that the medium must have got her dated mixed up: it was three days to her father's birthday. After the service Amy took Sadie, an elderly church member, home in the car. As they drove down the road from the church they met an ambulance, with flashing blue lights and sirens wailing. As there was an ambulance station nearby, this was not an uncommon sight, so both Sadie and Amy said a little prayer for the person in the ambulance.

Sadie invited Amy in, and she stayed for a while, helping the old woman to put her late husband's photograph into a locket. Sadie was lonely, and loath to allow company to leave, so Amy stayed and talked for a while. Eventually, she made her excuses, and went home, where she found Geoff pacing the floor, a worried look on his face.

*"You've got to go to the hospital straight away,"* he said. *Teresa's been taken in. Her waters have broken."*

Amy telephoned the hospital to see what was happening, and was told that Teresa was in labour. She left immediately, and reached the hospital in time to see her grandson born.

Daniel was born just before ten that night. Now the message made sense! The medium had not got the date wrong at all! She was telling Amy that it was Daniel's birthday!

Daniel was three weeks premature, and spent the first month of his life in hospital. Because of her problems with her neighbours, Teresa and Daniel stayed with Amy until the council allocated her another house. The new house needed decorating, which Teresa did herself, and she was eager to move in.

Everything went well until she began to hear loud noises in the new house. She was also aware of a presence. Daniel seemed to be able to see the presence, for he often looked past his mother and smiled, as if someone was there. Sometimes he would turn his head, as if someone was calling his name, then smile. He was five months old when matters escalated. Teresa rang Amy. She was in tears and frantic, saying she had to get out of the house.

That morning, Carolyn had visited Teresa and they both heard a loud banging in the front bedroom. They went into the hall, and the noise increased. Daniel was asleep in the back bedroom, and both women were amazed that the noise had not woken him up. Carolyn was afraid to go upstairs, but Teresa braved the noise and brought her son into the living room. Carolyn was terrified by now, as the banging continued. She made her excuses and left Teresa and Daniel alone.

Amy told Teresa not to worry, and that she would sort things out. First, she telephoned Pauline, who had returned from Saudi Arabia and bought a house a few miles from Teresa. When she heard what had happened, she offered to transport Teresa and Daniel to Amy's house.

When she heard this Amy telephoned Beth and asked her to help. Beth knew of a couple who would be able to help, but who would need transport. That evening, Amy collected the couple and Beth then returned home to pick up Teresa and Daniel before heading to Teresa's house.

The couple, Ann and Charles, went into the house alone, saying they were going to 'sweep' it for vibrations. They came out, saying that they could not pick anything up. They asked everyone to go into the living room, where they told Amy to take Daniel while Ann linked with Teresa.

Ann gave a little cry, and said that the presence was with Teresa, who looked terrified when she heard this. Ann assured her that no harm would come to her, and asked her spirit helpers to step forward to make contact with the spirit. At the same time, Amy and Beth asked their spirit friends to help also. Dan sat bolt upright in his grandmother's arms, clutching her coat with one hand. His pale blue eyes were like saucers as he stared, unblinking, at his mother. Ann began to shake then she spoke. The words she uttered helped Amy to identify the spirit.

*"Why are they locking me in the wall?"* she cried. *"Don't let them put me back in the wall."*

Everyone was aware of the anguish in the medium's voice.

*"They are stabbing me again,"* Ann went on. *"Why are they stabbing me?"*

Amy knew then that the spirit was Daniel's paternal grandmother. She had passed over two years previously and had left her body to medical research. She had been a materialistic, bitter woman who had disliked Teresa intensely. Amy was not surprised to find that this woman had stayed near her body and had witnessed it being stored in a walled cabinet until needed, then 'operated' on by student doctors.

She did not say anything, for she did not want to influence the medium, but as Ann brought more evidence, Amy became convinced that the spirit really was Daniel's other grandmother. Daniel's eyes never left the medium as he clung to his grandmother's coat.

Gently, Ann spoke to the spirit through her guide and helpers and explained that she should now pass on into the spirit world, where she would receive the care and healing she needed.

*"Can I have one last look at the child, and bid him farewell?"* the spirit asked, speaking through Ann. Ann turned then looked at Daniel, who smiled broadly. Then he raised his hand and waved

goodbye to his grandmother.

Daniel could not have known what the medium was saying when she used the word 'farewell'. Amy believed that he had seen what they had not, and he knew that the woman Ann was trying to help was someone who had been close to him since his birth.

Amy wondered if she had been wise to take Daniel into the house while Ann was working. She thought that the others, who were more experienced, would have instructed her to leave him outside if it was wrong for him to be present. The experience did not seem to harm him, and the child was given the opportunity to say goodbye to his grandmother, who had obviously visited him many times in his short life. Many years later she realised that she should not have taken Daniel into the house. Like many people, she made the mistake of believing that those with more experience than she had knew what they were doing.

Often, when a spirit is present in a home, no attempt is made to contact it other than to tell it to go away. Occasionally a priest, or vicar, may be called in to perform an 'exorcism'. Amy often wondered how these men could be qualified to do this, as they do not believe in the communication between discarnate and incarnate beings. A house may often become quiet after one of these 'exorcisms', but has the spirit actually gone? Will it be enough just to tell it to go?

Usually, when a spirit does not immediately pass on, there is a reason. They may be tied to the earth by their materialistic outlook and a desire to stay near their earthly homes and possessions. Others, especially in the case of a sudden passing, may not realise that their body has died and try to exist as they had done. These spirits must be confused when the majority of people they try to communicate with either do not hear, or react fearfully. No wonder they resort to moving objects around, or rapping to attract attention.

These spirits need help, and there are mediums, like Ann and Charles, who are able to communicate with them and explain to them that it is time to move on. Some term it 'rescue work', because they are rescuing souls from an unnatural existence between the two worlds, helping them on their journey to the place they have earned in the world of spirit.

These mediums are often also healers, or they will work with a healer. These two aspects of mediumship go hand in hand, for healing is often necessary before the spirit can pass on. It takes a special type of person to be able to deal with the problems of this work, for they have to deal with the problems of both the earthbound spirit and the people who are affected by its presence.

However, not all disturbances in the home are due to spirits. Sometimes there is a perfectly natural cause for them, such as bad plumbing, subsidence, mice etc. On talking to mediums who do this work, I find they all agree that a proportion of people who call them out to deal with psychic phenomena are seeking attention for themselves. There may be a presence in the house, or the person living there may be a psychic, and unable to recognise or control their gift. Either way, there are those who like to be different. They may call a medium out, but what they really want is to identify the spirit and for the 'haunting' to continue. As long as it does they remain 'different', and are the centre of attention.

There are cases where people experiment with ouija boards. Low spirits are often attracted by these contraptions, and can frighten those present. Just because we pass into spirit, it does not follow that we automatically become angels. As we could see with Daniel's grandmother, some spirits cling to their materialistic way of life and stay on a low level instead of progressing to a more spiritual life. Those who regard the ouija board as a party game are totally unqualified to handle such spirits.

Amy could not speak with any authority on this type of work, having never done it herself. However, she has spoken to mediums who do, and witnessed them working without being tempted to try it herself. At that moment in her life she was happy to know how it worked, but to leave it to others more qualified, and more willing to do this work than she was.

# Chapter Fourteen

Tim was fifteen and a half: old by any standards for a dog. In human years he would have been over a hundred. His eyesight had deteriorated, so he was almost blind and he had congestive heart disease. He received regular medication which affected his kidneys and he had to have a monthly injection for this. He was not incontinent, although when he had to go, he could not wait long. It was his coughing fits which were distressing, for they usually resulted in him collapsing in a seizure.

Amy agonised whether or not to put him to sleep, but he seemed to get so much out of life that she felt he deserved to live out his allotted spell. His seizures always seemed to affect her more than they did him and he recovered from them quickly.

The vet supported Amy's view, and was prepared to treat Tim as long as the dog's quality of life justified it. There were times, however, when Amy sat in his waiting room, her little dog clasped in her arms, fighting back her tears in case this was the day she would have to agree to put him to sleep.

If she was with Tim when he began to cough, she picked him up and laid him on his side on a footstool, then passed her hands over him in an attempt to calm him. Within a few moments his coughing ceased, he would become relaxed, and fall into a deep sleep. When he woke he was his old chirpy self and seemed none the worse for his attack.

He was her shadow and clung to her more than ever before. Wherever she went he was a step behind her. He lay under her desk as she worked in her study and on an old settee cushion by her bed at night. Although he was virtually blind he could always find her, wherever she was in the house.

Sometimes he became worse during the night and on these occasions she did her best to make sure he was comfortable. One night she woke because his breathing was noisy. She placed her hand on his chest and felt his lungs crackling like brown paper as he breathed. She automatically asked her spirit friends to help. The answer came to her immediately and she knew she should reduce the water in his body. She took him downstairs and put him into the front garden. He took two steps and began to urinate. She shivered on the doorstep in her nightdress for what seemed like hours. When she took him upstairs again his breathing was better, and he went off to sleep as soon as she put him on his cushion. She got into bed and turned onto her stomach so that she could stroke him with her right hand. After a while she looked down to see how he was. Her hand was glowing red in the gloom of the winter dawn, as if it was lit from the inside. She could see the shape of her finger bones against the bright, transparent flesh. She took this as a sign that he was receiving healing energies from the spirit world.

After his fifteenth birthday every day was a bonus for Tim, especially as his good days outnumbered his bad. However, no matter how many good days they have, old dogs only do one thing: they die. Amy knew that she would have to face the time when this would happen, and made the most of each day they had left together.

Christmas that year was busy, and they had a few visitors. As Amy tidied the house, she sorted through the dressing table drawers, throwing out a number of empty foil envelopes which had contained HRT patches. On the second of January, she was booked to take a service in a nearby church and decided to wear her gold Star of David. She could not find it, so wore something else.

Teresa, Daniel and their two dogs, Wilma and Pebbles, had stayed with Amy during the holidays, so she gave them a lift home before she went to church. They had a coffee, and chatted then Amy left, only to find that she could not start the car. She eventually had to get a taxi to take her to the church, and a friend, whom Teresa had telephoned, promised to fix the car and pick her up after the service. However, when Amy tried to go home, the car still would not start, and eventually it had to be towed before she could drive it home. She was over an hour late when she arrived home, and Geoff met her at the door.

*"Tim's dead,"* he said. *"He died twenty minutes ago."*

He explained that Tim had gone into the garden with Meg and Dolly. The two bitches came in after a few minutes, but Tim stayed outside, wandering around, picking up the small pieces of Christmas cake which had thrown out for the birds. He was determined to eat every little crumb because Geoff had to call him three times before the little villain finally came indoors, skipping like a puppy over the threshold. As he entered the living room he began to cough and retch, then fell on his side. He was dead.

His body was still warm when Amy took him into her arms and buried her face in his coat. She knew that all she held was an empty shell and that her little dog was gone, but she had to hold him close in one last hug, saying her belated goodbye. Geoff was apologetic, as if he felt responsible for Tim dying while Amy was out.

It was dark outside and the ground was frozen, so Geoff could not dig a grave in the garden at that time of night. That left them with the problem of what to do with Tim's body. Although Amy knew that he could no longer experience heat or cold, she could not face the idea of putting him in the garage overnight. Geoff covered the settee with strong plastic sheeting then placed a thick towel on top and laid Tim on it. They covered him with another towel and he lay there until morning.

They were in the process of planting a leylandi hedge in the front garden, buying one or two trees as they could afford them. Amy thought it was best that Tim lay between two of these trees, where he would not be disturbed.

As a Spiritualist, Amy thought she would have been able to accept

Tim's passing as a part of his life, but she found that her grief blotted everyone out, including her spirit friends. She withdrew into herself and was unable to come to terms with her loss. She could not talk about him for months without dissolving into tears, and her heart ached for her faithful companion. She had never grieved for anyone as she did for Tim. They had been the nearest thing a person and her dog could get to being soul mates and had understood each other. There was never any pretence between them, they accepted each other for what they were, their love unaffected by each other's mistakes and shortcomings. Amy reasoned with herself that he had lived a long and happy life, and had passed over quickly after pursuing his favourite hobby - eating something meant for someone else.

The relationship between people and their pets, especially dogs, is unique. A dog will give himself to you unconditionally. You never need to make excuses to him, because he will always forgive, whatever you have done or neglected to do. When you return home you are always sure he will be glad to see you. Should human companions betray you, he will comfort you and remain steadfastly loyal. The grief Amy felt for Tim's passing was for her own loss, and the knowledge that she could never replace the bright little soul who'd been her companion for more than fifteen years.

Unfortunately, not everyone understands how strong the bond between a person and his dog can be, and consequently do not give the bereaved owner the support he needs. Amy was constantly told that she should get another dog immediately.

Amy is a great believer in getting back onto a horse after you have fallen off, but she could not see how getting another dog would ease her loss. She was surrounded with dogs, each one an individual with their own personalities and characteristics, some of which they had inherited from Tim. They were his son, daughter, granddaughter and great granddaughter respectively. She loved them all, and they loved her back, but none of them was Tim.

About ten days later, Beth telephoned.

*"I visited you last night,"* she said. *"You were sobbing in your sleep. Your shoulders were shaking."*

Amy knew that there was no point in denying this, but she was perturbed that Beth had entered her bedroom uninvited. The fact that she had done so to ease a friend's pain did not matter. Amy is very old fashioned, and believes that people should wait until they are asked. She is also a coward, and did not want to say anything to Beth in case it hurt her feelings. Amy finds it hard to say 'no', so when Beth indicated that she would 'visit' her again that night, she could not find an excuse to put her off. Geoff is not a Spiritualist, so she felt that she did not have the right to invite a third person into their bedroom, even if she would only be there in spirit.

As the day wore on, Amy regretted being so weak. Beth had always been an understanding person and would not have been upset if she had explained how she felt. Amy went to bed early that night and meditated before she went to sleep, asking Mr. Latimer not to allow Beth into the bedroom that night. Confident that Beth would not 'visit' her bedroom, Amy slept soundly, and did not wake up when Geoff came to bed.

She woke in the middle of the night with an unpleasant feeling in her head. Her skull felt as if it would burst with the pressure from inside. She tried to relax, thinking this would ease the stress, but it did not. Her head was like a balloon blown up to its limit, and she was afraid it would explode. A sound, rather like a hand being dragged over the surface of an inflated balloon, filled her ears, and she panicked. Then she heard herself say, "All right. I'll come with you."

The pressure fell away, and she relaxed. She found herself in a calm soothing place, and was glad that she had ceased to resist. Then she realised that she was in Beth's bedroom, sitting beside her on the bed. All she could remember thinking was that she was concerned because she was naked.

Amy has no further recollection of what happened that night and was not aware of returning to her own bed, but when she woke the next morning she felt more relaxed than she had been since

Tim had passed away. Geoff commented on how well she looked and attributed it to an early night. For the first time in two weeks she had not kept him awake by tossing and turning in her sleep.

She was confused, and felt that she could not confide in anyone. Had she really gone to Beth's house? If so, why could she remember nothing other than sitting on her friend's bed? Was it a dream, brought about by the suggestion that Beth was coming to help her? Personally, I do not think that this was the case. She firmly believed that Beth could not enter the bedroom that night, because Mr. Latimer and Grey Wolf were always there, and would have respected her wishes. She had fallen asleep, safe in the knowledge that she would not be disturbed. Beth telephoned her later that day to see how she was feeling. Amy did not mention her experience, but admitted that she felt much better.

*"I thought you might,"* said Beth, *"But I had a difficult job, because Mr. Latimer would not allow me anywhere near you. I asked my guide to have a word with him, and they agreed that you would benefit from healing, so they brought you to my house."*

Beth's unprompted statement was enough to confirm to Amy that she had not dreamed the incident. She had always tried to be analytical when things like this happened to her and tried to look at them without her Spiritualist beliefs colouring her reasoning. Others may come to a different conclusion, but they were not there. They did not experience it. Amy did, and she did not feel that she had imagined any part of it. If she had, then Beth must have had an identical experience, because she described all that Amy remembered without being prompted.

Whether Amy did have an out of body experience, or whether it was the power of suggestion which prompted and fuelled her imagination, we shall never know. Whatever it was, it happened exactly as I have described it. The most important outcome of this episode was that Amy did feel much better the next morning. She still missed her little dog, but her life was no longer on hold. She was going forward again.

However well meaning Beth was, Amy felt that she had invaded her privacy and should not have visited her as she did, especially the first time, without asking first. Mediums should have principles. The more developed their mediumship becomes, the greater their responsibilities are. Being able to do these things does not mean that you should do them. Discretion and common courtesy should always be observed.

We all long to see our loved ones again after they pass over, just to reassure ourselves that their spirits really have survived the death of their physical bodies. The closer our relationship, the more we expect them to come forward to give us this reassurance. Amy half expected to see Tim, or be aware of him, but she was never sure that she did. Sometimes, as she sat at her desk, she felt he might have been there in his usual place, by her feet, but she could not be sure that this was not wishful thinking on her part.

She still had not found her Star of David. Where could it be? She turned the house inside out, but could not find it. She had never worn much jewellery, but had felt an urge to buy this soon after she began to take services. As far as she knew, none of her spirit helpers had been Jewish in their earthly existence, so it was unlikely that any of them had influenced her to buy it. It was a nice piece of jewellery, and she had enjoyed wearing it.

Then she remembered that she had wound the chain around the star and placed it in a used foil HRT envelope to prevent it from becoming tangled. She could clearly remember patting it closed, then putting it into her dressing table drawer. Horrified, she recalled throwing a number of used HRT envelopes out before Christmas, some of which had been in the drawer. A further search of the bedroom revealed nothing, and she had to face the fact that she had accidentally thrown the star out.

Teresa could see how upset her mother was, and she conducted a thorough, disciplined search of the house. She searched both upstairs and downstairs, in the car, in all Amy's handbags and the pockets of all her clothes. Methodically, she searched the dining room, beginning with the dresser drawers, which she emptied onto the table, examining the contents before putting them back. There was no sign of the Star of David, with or without its foil envelope. The whole house got the same treatment, and she looked in places that Amy had already searched. When she had finished, Amy had to admit that it was really lost, and she forgot about it. There were more pressing things to occupy her mind.

Dolly became sick in March. She had been fine on Sunday evening before Amy left for her service. Sadie was going with her, as she had never attended that particular church. (It was Sadie's ambition to visit every Spiritualist church in the area) Dolly had fawned over the old woman, as usual. She always made sure that she had more than her fair share of attention from any visitor.

After they left, Dolly had gone into the garden with Meg, her daughter. When she came back into the house, she began to vomit. Amy took her to the vet the following day, but she deteriorated rapidly, and had to be admitted to the vetinary hospital.

It took Dolly nearly a week to die. She had been poisoned, and her death was very painful. What made it worse was that she had spent the last days of her life in a cage in the hospital, feeling that she had been abandoned by those she loved most. Although Amy visited her, she seemed to pick the times when Dolly was unconscious. Other times, she rang to check on Dolly's condition, and was distressed to hear her barking and digging at the door of her cage in an effort to escape.

A post mortem revealed that her organs had been badly damaged by the poison, and she could not have been saved. In hindsight, it would have been better to put her to sleep immediately, but on the evidence she was presented with at the time, Amy had to make an effort to save her.

Someone had deliberately put food into the garden, laced with a common household product, which had been palatable. It could not have got into the garden accidentally, because it would normally have been kept at the back of the house, and well away from food. Because Dolly's early symptoms were so similar to Tim's, it was a real possibility that he had also been poisoned, but had died immediately because of his weak heart. Only Meggie escaped, probably because she was such a fussy eater.

Amy could not believe that such a bright, lively soul could have been extinguished: the vitality and energy she had seen in Dolly's eyes before she left for her service could surely not be lost forever. It had to continue in another form. One minute she was pressing herself against Sadie, like a cat demanding to be stroked then she was vomiting her insides out.

The loss of two dogs within three months knocked Amy for six. It was like losing two of her children. She needed help just to cope, but nobody other than Beth seemed to understand.

Although she was a family pet, Dolly had been Susan's dog. Or rather, Susan had been Dolly's special person. That little dog lived for the time when her mistress came home at weekends from boarding school, and would have nothing to do with anyone while Susan was around. When Susan went away to work, Dolly slipped into a routine of being a family dog until they were reunited.

Susan later mentioned that sometimes she felt that Dolly had jumped onto her bed, as she had done when she was alive. She asked her mother why Dolly should be with her, when she lived nearly three hundred miles away, somewhere Dolly had never visited. Amy replied that now Dolly was where she wanted to be. She was unable to be with Susan all of the time while she had inhabited a physical body. Now she had shed that body and she had no such restrictions. She could be with the one she loved most.

Dolly did not desert the rest of the family entirely, for Amy was frequently aware of her, usually when she was upset or needed help. She wondered why Dolly should visit so soon after her death, and yet Tim had not. Each of the dogs had their own member of the family to whom they had chosen as their 'special' person, and Amy belonged to Tim. So why was she not aware of him? She would not find the answer to this question for seven years.

# Chapter Fifteen

It was a chance remark by a church member which brought Harry, her childhood sweetheart, back into Amy's mind. She had not heard from him since they were teenagers, although her mother had met him on social occasions and had relayed his best wishes to her. All she knew was that he had got married and had children.

She had spoken to Harry's younger brother, Andy on a number of occasions without recognising who he was. Andy had been a young schoolboy when she had last seen him, as he was quite a few years younger than her. When she realised who he was she telephoned him and laughingly told him off for not identifying himself to her. Then she said the words which would change the next months of her life.

*"How is Harry?"*

*"He's just been admitted to hospital,"* replied Andy. *"He was found in a collapsed state in his house."*

*"Would anyone mind if I went to see him?"* she asked.

*"There's nothing to stop you from visiting him, although he won't recognise you,"* he replied. *"He doesn't know where he is, he's suffering from some sort of dementia. His partner left him a couple of months ago and he's been on his own ever since. I'm the only one who visits him"*

Amy asked Geoff if he would mind if she visited Harry, and he said he did not, so the next day she went to the hospital to see him. He was asleep when she arrived, so she sat at his bedside until he woke. He looked at her, and she could see that he was trying to remember where he had seen her before.

*"You don't recognise me, do you?"* she asked.

He stared at her for some time without answering. She took hold of his hand, mentally asking for healing for him. Then she saw a light of intelligence and recognition in his eyes.

*"You're Amy,"* he said, and mentioned her maiden name to further identify her. *"I should have married you a long time ago."*

Andy had arrived by then, and was surprised to find Harry looking so bright and interested in what was going on. Amy took her leave of them, saying that she would come back the next day, which was Sunday.

She told Geoff about Harry's condition, and how she was concerned that he was so confused. Geoff, remembering his time in that same hospital, urged her to cook the Sunday joint that day so that she could make sandwiches to take in for Harry.

*"The food in that hospital is rubbish,"* he said, *"and the portions aren't enough to feed a bird, never mind a grown man."*

Amy put the leg of pork in the oven after tea. It was a large joint and took a long time to cook. Geoff went to bed before it was ready to come out of the oven. Amy sat watching the television, but she felt that someone was poking her in the back.

*"Make him some rock buns,"* a voice said in her head. *"He loves rock buns."*

Amy knew that it was Harry's mother who was putting this into her mind. She made a batch of rock buns and put them in the oven with the pork. The next day Harry enjoyed pork and stuffing sandwiches and rock buns.

*"They're my favourite,"* he said. *"How did you know that?"*

Amy nearly told him that Lizzie, his mother had suggested the rock buns, but she knew little about Harry and his beliefs, so thought it wise not to say anything.

She visited regularly, and soon was aware that there was a rift between Andy and two young women who also visited. These were Harry's ex partner's daughters, and he loved them as his own.

They were also very fond of him and were concerned for his state of health.

They had good reason to be, for scans and tests revealed that he was suffering from motor neurone disease and a form of dementia.

Amy's own health was not very good, either. She was suffering from a thyroid goitre which had suddenly begun to grow at quite an alarming rate. Her doctor arranged for her to see a specialist, and she obtained an appointment within two weeks of being referred.

Harry loved reading westerns, but he had no spectacles. Andy informed Amy that Harry had ordered some and they were waiting to be collected. The stumbling block was that they would cost nearly a hundred pounds, and Harry had no money.

Working on her grandmother's principle of shy bairns getting nowt, Amy telephoned the optician and explained Harry's situation. They were very sympathetic, especially when Amy explained that his condition was terminal. She cried when they rang her back and asked her to call in for them free of charge. Her faith in human nature got a big boost that day.

Harry was a difficult patient because he absconded from the hospital on a number of occasions in an attempt to return home. The doctors recommended that he should go to a secure unit where he could be cared for. On the day before Christmas Eve he was moved to a home for the elderly mentally infirm. He was fifty six on January the first.

Amy was horrified. She was not allowed to see him on the day he was moved, but was told she could visit on Christmas Day and take him out if necessary. She bought small presents for Harry to give to his adopted daughters and their children as well as for his neighbour. On Christmas morning she collected Harry and took him to see one of his daughters and then his neighbour before returning him to the home for Christmas lunch. Sadly she had to leave him there and went home herself to start her own Christmas.

Amy took Harry to see his sister on his birthday and spent the day with her, catching up on old times. Harry enjoyed himself, and it was a pleasure to see him lose the vacant look that he had while in the home.

Amy went to see the specialist and he said that she should have surgery immediately to remove the goitre. She was both relieved and worried. Relieved because something was going to be done about her illness and worried when the surgeon asked for a needle biopsy. She was also concerned about Harry. Apart from his ex wife, who had begun to visit him weekly, he had very few visitors other than herself.

She took him home that weekend and introduced him to Geoff. Harry's clothes were filthy and smelled bad, so she gave him a bath and washed his clothes. Geoff loaned him some clothes while his were drying. When he ate his meals, Amy noticed that he had trouble swallowing. She knew that this was something that happened with motor neurone disease and pointed this out to the nurse on duty when she took Harry back.

Amy soon realised that this particular home was not the place for Harry. He was very unhappy, and tried to escape on a number of occasions. There was nothing she could do about this, for she was not related to him. Nevertheless, she tried, only to be put in her place by those in control of the home. The home was always understaffed, and the standards of hygiene were poor. Much was left to the carers, who were unqualified staff working on very low wages. They had no idea of barrier nursing, so consequently, when a bug got into the home not many of the residents escaped it.

Amy worried what would happen to Harry while she was in hospital, for her daily visits stimulated his mind and he became more able to carry on a conversation. She decided that she would telephone him every evening while she was unable to visit and hope that he would realise that he had not been abandoned. It hurt her to hear the despair in his voice as they spoke, especially when one evening he cried.

*"Amy, rescue me, please."*

She was unable to visit him for just over two weeks, and when she returned she was saddened to see that he was sedated to make him more manageable following more attempts to escape.

It became very hard to continue to visit, but she knew that if she did not go to see him he would only get a brief visit from his ex wife once a week. Harry hated these visits, but there was nothing he could do to stop this good lady who was doing her duty as she saw it.

On the occasions when she visited Harry during meal times, he was allowed to have his meal in his room. She noticed that he was still on a normal diet, and pointed out to the carer that he was unable to swallow his food. The carer said that she would pass this information on.

Harry's room was in a bad condition, and it smelled really badly. The bedding was not changed often enough and Amy pointed this out to the home manager, who said she would rectify the situation. There was no improvement, so Amy reported the home to the local authority. They had a surprise visit from an inspector, who agreed with Amy that the home had shortcomings. After this visit Amy noticed that Harry was sleeping a lot and he seemed to be heavily sedated while she was there.

As Easter approached Amy was having trouble with her car and could not visit for a couple of days. When she saw him on Easter Sunday she knew that he was very ill. The nurse had told her that Harry had 'a bit of an infection' when she entered the home, but that was not how she found him. As she entered the room, two young carers were struggling to dress Harry, who was emaciated by now. He had diarrhoea, and had All Bran in his mouth, which he had tried to feed himself with. His head fell forward and the All Bran spilled down his shirt. He was sweating profusely and was obviously very ill. One of the carers went to fetch another shirt, while the other sat Harry on the en suite toilet because he had soiled his pants.

*"Can I help?"* asked Amy. *"He might be better with someone he knows."*

*"He won't know who you are,"* the young lad replied. *"So I*

don't think it will make much difference."

*"He will know me,"* insisted Amy. *"I visit him regularly."*

Harry reached out and put his arms around Amy's waist.

*"You're Amy,"* he said, *"and I should have married you years ago."*

Amy cradled Harry's head to her chest, feeling his sweat seep through her clothes. She was going to have to take charge. It was not fair on the two young people, who were obviously untrained and unprepared for the situation they found themselves with..

"*Why don't you just let him go back to bed,"* she said. "*Put some protection on him and let him sleep if he wants to. He's in no condition to be out of bed.*

Thankful that someone was directing them, they helped her to put him to bed then left. She sat on his bed and took his hand. His breathing was laboured and his eyes were protruding. Nevertheless, he was able acknowledge her by squeezing her hand.

"Would you like me to play some music?*" she asked.*

*He* nodded, and she sought a tape out which she knew he liked and played it. She sat next to him, wiping the sweat from his brow. He reached out for her hand and grasped it, surprising her by the firmness of his grip. Then he looked at her. She smiled at him, then realised that he was now looking over her shoulder, as if someone was standing behind her. He seemed to recognise whoever it was, and Amy knew that Lizzie, his mother, had come for him. He squeezed her hand once more then stopped breathing.

She did not feel sad at his passing, but relieved that he was no longer suffering. She sat with him for a few moments, making sure that he really had gone, then went to find the nurse in charge. He was on the telephone. She asked if he would come and look at Harry, but he waved her away.

*"Five minutes,"* he called to her.

Amy went back to the room, passing a toilet on the way. A senior carer was scrubbing the toilet, wearing a pair of rubber gloves as a token gesture to barrier nursing.

*"I think that Harry has stopped breathing,"* she said to him.

The carer dropped what he was doing and followed her into Harry's room. He flicked Harry's eyes, but he did not respond. Amy knelt by the bed and prayed. The carer brought the nurse, who ordered Amy to leave. She did. Her work was done. Harry had gone with his mother and there was nothing they could do to him now.

As always, Geoff was a tower of strength, and listened while Amy told him what had happened. He was relieved that her ordeal was over, for the months of caring for Harry had taken a heavy toll on her health. He knew that it would take some time, but he was there every moment as she took the home to task and made a written complaint about Harry's treatment while in their care. Her complaint was upheld, and there were 'considerable staff changes' as a result.

Amy wondered if she had really done her best for Harry, whether she could have been more forceful and persisted with her complaints about his treatment. She blamed herself for not doing enough, for allowing the staff at the home to bully her because she was not a relative.

"*You helped him,"* said Geoff. *"You made a difference in his life. Without you he would have died alone and unloved. Remember what you did for him, and don't beat yourself up thinking you could have done more, because you couldn't."*

This episode in her life often came back to Amy, but with Geoff beside her she successfully placed it behind her.

# Chapter Sixteen

Just when she thought that things could not get any worse, they did. Susan telephoned to say that she had been feeling ill, and had to attend a hospital for tests. It was possible that she might have a brain tumour, and she needed details of the nature of the tumour which her father had had removed. Amy was devastated. Susan was only twenty three, with her whole life ahead of her. How could this happen to someone who was so fit and active? What made her feel worse was that she could not be with Susan at this time. She asked friends, both in spirit and on the earth, to send healing for Susan, and to help her to cope.

Amy has had times in her life when she has been at a low ebb, but none had ever compared with this. She had not recovered from the loss of her two dogs and her spirits had been low before Susan broke the news. That night she asked Mr. Latimer and Grey Wolf to help her to cope. Her faith was being tested to the limit. If there really was a spirit world, and a God, she needed a sign to comfort and fortify her.

The next morning she received a gas bill which was outrageously high. Although she had made regular payments, they said she owed a lot of money and her payments would increase from seven pounds a week to twenty six. As if she had not enough to worry about! How on earth could she afford that? Then she noticed that the reading was estimated and calmed down. She decided to check the meter herself and looked for the key which opened the box outside the front door, where it was situated. The key was not in its usual place, so she began to look elsewhere for it. The first place she tried was the left hand drawer of the dresser. Lying on top of everything else, as if it had just been placed there, was her Star of David.

How had it found its way into the drawer? It certainly had not been there the day before, because Amy had put something away in the drawer. She wondered if this could be the sign that she had asked for. Could her spirit friends have returned the lost jewellery to her? As far as she was concerned, it had been thrown out in December and was in a bin bag somewhere on a rubbish tip. The dresser drawer had been thoroughly searched, and had been used almost daily without anyone discovering the jewellery. Amy investigated further, but could find no feasible explanation. She had to conclude that her spirit friends had returned her lost Star of David as the sign that she had asked for. Later that day Susan telephoned to say that the tests were negative and she did not have a brain tumour.

Objects which are transported through physical matter by psychic energy are known as apports. These often appear in physical circles where a group of people sit regularly with a physical medium. These apports are often flowers, though there is documented evidence of all sorts of small objects appearing in the séance room.

We may also experience apports during our everyday lives without recognising them for what they are. We may notice an unfamiliar object and wonder where it came from, and who brought it into our home, but usually, we will find that an object, which normally resides in one room, appears in another without anyone moving it. Only when you become aware that this phenomenon is possible, can you recognise it when it happens, and it is surprising how often it occurs.

The next time Amy consciously recognised an apport was quite spectacular. She was typing letters for the church onto her word processor, and disagreed with the committee's stand on one particular matter. She had to send this letter, which had been dictated to her by the committee, to a church member and it saddened her to have to do so. After printing the letter out she swung away from her desk in her revolving chair to read it. She felt that the member was being unjustly reprimanded and that the punishment was far greater than it should have been. Her feelings ran high at the attitude the committee was taking, felt they were acting in an unspiritual way, and were influenced by personal opinions rather than evidence.

As she turned back to the word processor to print out a second copy, she noticed a card of fuse wire lying across the top of the machine, half covering the space where the paper was fed through. The card was very old and covered in dust. It held fuse wire of different sizes, the smallest being very fine. This was unwound, and the end was sticking out like a fine silver antenna.

How had the card appeared? Where had it come from? Dumfounded, she stared up at the ceiling, as if she expected to get the answer from above. If it had fallen, then surely it would have made a sound as it landed. She had heard nothing, despite being only inches away from the machine. It could not have been there earlier, because it covered the space where the letter she had been reading had passed through. There was no one else in the room and Amy had never seen the card of wire before. It was very old fashioned, possibly dating back to the 1940's. She would have certainly remembered it being in the study.

She rang a few friends, and asked their opinion. One or two suggestions seemed likely and were on the same lines of the conclusions she had come to. Perhaps her spirit friends had been concerned that she had become annoyed with what she was having to type, and had decided to leave her a message. One suggested that it meant that she was being told not to blow a fuse. Another was that, because the thin wire was unwound, she should be careful not to have a short fuse. Both seemed possible explanations. If it was a message from her spirit friends, then she should listen. Was that what it was? Amy will never know, and still wonders if the card of wire really was an apport. If it was, who sent it? Whoever was responsible, they were aware of her feelings, because the wire appears to have been significant.

There is always a possibility that we may blame any unexplained sound or happening on spirit intervention. Most knocks which occur in the middle of the night, or objects appearing in a place they are not normally kept, have a simple explanation. When Amy first heard the rappings which appeared to come from the wooden headboard, she did not associate them with spirit communication. She thought it was because the temperature had dropped, and the headboard was cracking, similar to the way a radiator makes noises as it cools. It was only afterwards, when she learned more about psychic phenomena, and heard the rappings again, that she connected them to the spirit world.

She has regularly experienced so-called phenomena in circles and in her home, and thought she was seeing or hearing spirit people. Then, when she investigated, she found that it was a trick of the light, or a creaky chair. The majority of these noises or sightings usually have an explanation which has nothing to do with psychic phenomena. It is always best to investigate and eliminate all other possible sources of 'phenomena' before attributing it to the spirit world.

She had heard of other people experiencing knockings and attributing them to spirit without a proper investigation. There is a well known tale of a circle which had been set up in a church that regularly heard a tapping noise as they sat in a darkened room. The circle leader would say, "Welcome, friend," every time she heard this, but never got a reply. Then a visitor heard the noise and investigated it. He discovered that the church was infested with death watch beetles, and it was these that the circle leader had been welcoming as friends.

I am still not sure whether Amy's ground glass pelican, which was on the window sill of her study, was manipulated by spirit intervention, or if there was some quite ordinary explanation for its behaviour. You may well wonder why I have used the word behaviour concerning an inanimate object, but it proved to be active, thus behaving very strangely, over a period of days.

She had just purchased the pelican, and was very pleased with it. It was made from opaque ground glass, and was reminiscent of

Rene Lalique's work. Perhaps it was by Lalique, although it was highly unlikely. It certainly did not bear his signature. If it had been by him she had found a real bargain, although neither its maker nor its value interested her. She had bought it because she liked it.

The pelican fascinated her and she handled it constantly, as you do with a new possession, admiring the workmanship. She placed it on the window sill in her study so that she could look at it while she worked. It caught the light, and seemed to take on a different hue according to the time of day and the weather. Although it was naturally colourless, or perhaps, a neutral shade of grey, it ranged from grey to blue, then lilac, and often, a rosy pink or pale lemon. Sometimes it changed colour as Amy worked, as if it was reflecting her moods. It faced to the left, in a position where the light shone through it, making it glow with the colour it was reflecting at that moment.

Amy's study was a no-go area and nobody entered it unless invited to do so. There was nothing in there to interest anyone but her, and she had her own filing system, which involved heaps of papers, manuscripts and documents lying on every available flat surface, including the floor. The effect suggested chaos, but she was always able to locate anything she needed. There were pictures and posters on the wall, and small ornaments here and there which she enjoyed looking at while she searched for inspiration for her writing.

One day she noticed that the pelican was facing to the right. This annoyed her, for it meant that someone had been in her study and had handled the pelican. She knew she had not done it because she always faced her ornaments in the direction she felt they looked best. Grumbling under her breath, she put it back the way she liked it, and continued working until lunch time.

*"Why did you go into my study?"* she asked Geoff over lunch.

*"I haven't been anywhere near your precious study,"* he replied.

*"Somebody has, and there's been nobody in the house but the two of us,"* she said, *"I know, because the pelican was facing the wrong way. Somebody must have handled it."*

*"Don't look at me,"* he replied, then, with a laugh, *"Perhaps it was one of your spooky pals."*

*"So that's it!"* she said. *"You thought you'd play a joke. Well, it didn't work. I knew it was you all the time."*

Geoff began to laugh, and he shook his head. "Honestly, Amy, I haven't been in your study, and I definitely did not touch your pelican. I wish I had thought of it, it would have been a good joke!"

Amy had lived with Geoff for over twenty five years and by now she knew when he was joking and when he was being serious. However, the pelican had been moved, so if Geoff had not moved it, who had been in her study? She finished her meal and returned to her work. As she sat down she looked at the pelican. It was now facing her! She stared at it, astonished. Geoff had been downstairs with her all the time and there was nobody else in the house. How could it have moved? Who could have moved it?

Perhaps the heat of the sun through the window had created some sort of energy in the glass bird, causing it to rotate. Amy was not acquainted with matters of physics, so she could not understand why it could have happened. Yet the fact remained that it had moved, and there had been nobody in the room.

Was she mistaken? Had she accidentally moved the bird's position herself? She felt that there was an outside chance that this might be the case. She may have touched it while reaching for something else, although she could not remember doing so. To make sure that her memory was not playing tricks with her, she placed the pelican onto a circle of card, marking the position of his beak, and the time it had been there. This diagram proved to her conclusively that she was not imagining things. The pelican was moving in an anti-clockwise direction, completing a full circle in about a day and a half. It did this for a few days then stopped, only to start again periodically for a few more weeks.

I can offer no explanation as to how or why this happened. Perhaps the bird was moved by a spirit who wanted to make Amy aware of his presence. That would fit in with Amy's beliefs, and the other things which had happened to her in recent years. Then again, Geoff might have been the culprit, although that is highly unlikely. He could never resist owning up to a joke, usually in front of family or friends, so they could share in it. He has never done this.

Amy could not honestly say that she knew who had moved the bird, but she knew it had moved, whether by human, psychic or solar energy. Until she obtains evidence which offers a satisfactory explanation as to why the bird moved, and, incidentally, why it stopped moving, the revolving pelican must remain one of life's unsolved mysteries.

The second draft of her novel was finally finished and Amy telephoned her agent. He was a little cool towards her, and asked why it had taken her so long to complete. She explained that she had been ill, but his attitude puzzled her. She asked if he wanted to see the manuscript. He said he did, and she sent it off to him. It was another six weeks before the agent replied, and his reaction was not what Amy had hoped for. The manuscript still needed a lot of work, and for the first time, he criticized the story line. She was devastated. It was her first taste of rejection, and she found it a bitter pill to swallow. Dispirited, she put the book away and did not pick it up again for three years.

It was then that Amy was given a pile of writers' magazines. She scanned through them for articles which might help her with her writing. One of them contained an article which stated that her agent was looking for women who could write racy novels. He had discovered one writer who could do this, and her first novel had been a best seller. Amy realised that this man was too shrewd to have rejected her novel just because it did not contain the sexy dialogue which was now in vogue, but she did feel that this change of genre might have been contributory to his offhand manner when she had first telephoned him. She picked up her manuscript and read it again. Because she had not touched it for three years she was able to see it with new eyes.

Before she had read five chapters, she could see what he meant.

She had not edited the book very well. It had lost its flow and did not read as well as the first draft. There was nobody to blame but herself. She would have to take a more professional approach to her writing if she wanted to succeed.

There were other things more important at the moment, however. She had become a member of the Spiritualists National Union soon after she had first begun to take services. The Union has an education programme, which Amy had not known about until she read through some of the reports following the Union's AGM. She could not believe that the knowledge she craved had been there for the asking. Why had nobody told her?

She wasted no more time and applied for her first correspondence course. This was to be the first of many. The more she learned, the more she understood. This knowledge inspired her to learn more. She was inspired to teach, to pass the knowledge she had gained on to those who sought it. The opportunity came when she attended a meeting run by the district education committee at a local church, and was asked to form a development class in that church.

Because she was now teaching, she pressed on with her own education, and attended as many seminars as she could, making comprehensive and extensive notes so that she would not forget anything. One of the seminars she attended was run by the Noah's Ark Society, and dealt with physical phenomena. During this seminar she was told a tale of how one medium's husband was regularly transported from the séance room by psychic energy, and was found on his hands and knees on the lawn.

Amy did not know how true this could be, but allowed that it could happen and tucked it into her memory bank. Anecdotes like that one often came in handy to enliven a lecture or workshop.

This was a period Amy enjoyed, for she was teaching and learning at the same time. It was hard work, for although she ran the class on similar lines to Joseph's, she did not have the benefit of dedicated sitters to help to develop the students. That did not stop her students from progressing and it was a happy, light hearted, yet disciplined class. There were also some hilarious moments.

One of the exercises she set her class was for them to choose a piece of music which they thought described them as a person, then speak on it for five minutes. She had done this exercise herself in Joseph's class, and had enjoyed it. She showed the students what she wanted them to do by demonstrating her choice of music.

The first to attempt it was George, a Jamaican man about fifty years old. The following week he came prepared to work. He brought with him a black bin bag containing props and a folding table under his arm. He was smartly dressed in his best suit and immaculately groomed. The class sat in a semi circle, with Amy directly opposite the large lectern on the raised rostrum. George's girl friend arranged the props, which consisted of a large family Bible and a vase containing a single red rose. She then placed the tape in the tape machine before joining the rest of the class.

George mounted the rostrum and walked to the lectern, which he gripped firmly at each side. He peered over the top of it, looking down at the rest of the class.

*"This is my music,"* he said, his face deadly serious. He reminded Amy of a Baptist minister from the deep south of the USA.

It was a gentle, country ballad about a family Bible, and Amy settled in her chair to listen. She closed her eyes for a split second, although it was more like a blink, for she had to observe George as well as listen to his music.

When she opened her eyes she could not see George. He was gone! In that split second, in what was hardly more than a blink of the eyes, he had disappeared and was nowhere to be seen. He had not had time to leave the rostrum, so where could he be? Amy's thoughts went to the seminar she had attended. She knew she could not panic, but wild thoughts raced through her head.

*"He's gone!"* she gasped, and the church president, who was sitting beside her, looked puzzled. Amy tried to appear calm and in control of the situation, but inwardly she was panicking. What would she say to the head of the education committee, who had

appointed her as leader of the class? Would she have to report George's disappearance to the police, and if so, what on earth would she say? Should they look outside to see if he was there?

*"What's the matter?"* asked the president.

*"He's gone. He's disappeared!"* whispered Amy, not wishing to alarm the rest of the class, who were now becoming curious as to why their leader was so disturbed.

The president laughed, and pulled Amy to the left, where George was just visible. He had sat down in the split second that Amy's eyes had been closed. He was visible to everyone but Amy, as the lectern hid him from her view. The class thought it was a huge joke, and Amy, relieved that George had not been transported by spirits to another place, laughed with them. However, she did learn one thing from it. A little knowledge can be dangerous, and there was no substitute for experience.

She was also given another view of Spiritualism, surprisingly from the very person who had inspired her to rejoin the church. She had not seen that particular medium for some time. One Sunday night, when she was giving a service at a church, Amy noticed the medium sitting in the congregation. They spoke afterwards, and Amy found that the woman had been attending a university, where she was working on a degree in Theology. The change in her attitude puzzled Amy. One of the theories the woman put forward was that guides were not departed spirits, but alto egos of the medium. She also stated that, because Amy's guide and doorkeeper were both male, she was using them as a substitute for the male influences which had been missing in her life. Amy could not agree with this theory, but found that she was unable to offer any proof that Mr. Latimer and Grey Wolf were in fact spirits who helped and guided her through her life.

Even if she had been able to think of a way to defend her own belief, it would have been lost on this woman, who was full of her own new found knowledge, (based upon theories that others have written in books) and who refused to entertain any other possibility. Amy felt that this was a case of education narrowing rather than broadening the mind, and was sad to see the difference in the woman who had previously inspired her.

Amy wished she could have held her own in the theosophical debate with the woman, but her own knowledge was not great enough to do this. She was also appalled when the woman stated that she did not believe that when she had been working as a medium she was communing with the spirit world. She claimed that she had often drawn on her own experiences and some of the 'evidence' she had given was based on her own memories, coupled with intuition and a degree of psychic ability.

Amy could not get this woman out of her mind. The change in her was dramatic. She appeared to have no belief in anything; her head was filled with facts, figures and dates rather than what religion is based upon, which is fellowship and love. She regarded herself as an intellectual and lived by the statistics which she had committed to memory. Her mind was now closed: she had all the knowledge she needed to obtain her degree. There was nothing else to know.

It was after meeting this woman and while she was still leading the development class, that Amy decided to further her own education and discovered the delights of The Arthur Findlay College.

# Chapter Seventeen

As soon as you step through the door of The Arthur Findlay College, you become aware of the tremendous energy which has built up in it over many years of being the centre for psychic and spiritual studies. On her first visit to the college, Amy felt that she was where she needed to be. She was among like minded people who were all seeking knowledge and coming together in harmony. The college was full and the atmosphere both congenial and exciting. Her own course dealt with the phenomena of Spiritualism and was held over five days. This whetted her appetite for more knowledge and she returned to the college as soon and as often as she could afford to.

The college was bequeathed to The Spiritualist's National Union by J. Arthur Findlay in 1964. It comprises of a large country house on three floors which is set in its own grounds. Its location, next to Stansted Airport, makes it convenient for overseas as well as domestic students. The college is renowned for the quality of its cuisine and its wonderful atmosphere.

At one of the courses, which was at a reduced rate because it was designed to give student tutors experience, an announcement was made at the end of the course which inspired Amy. The speaker thanked the paying students for supporting the student tutors and stated that there was always a need for more tutors at the college. Everyone who felt they would like to join the course would be considered.

Amy tackled the speaker afterwards and she was given the name of the person who was in charge of the tutor training programme.

Every time she enquired about the course, she was asked what experience she had. She did not feel encouraged and felt that she was being told to go away and gain the experience. To do this she had to have the opportunity to teach and she was not being given it. She did not want to push herself forward, as she had seen others do, and canvas for seminars or workshops. Perhaps this was a mistake, for if people were not aware of her abilities and had not seen her work, why should they invite her to teach in their church?

She did manage to overcome this and two years later, with a lot of teaching in classes and seminars in her own area under her belt, she tried again. She was given a form to fill in, but was told that there was a long waiting list for the course, so there was no pressure to return it. She became despondent and felt that she would never get the opportunity to learn to be a 'proper' tutor. Then she met Sybil, who was to be her mentor.

Sybil believed in her and helped her to regain her self confidence and to value herself as a person. After attending one of Sybil's courses, Amy's ambitions to teach and to write about Spiritualism were re-kindled.

It was about this time that Amy started a home circle. It was not held in her own home, as she did not think that Geoff would approve, but at a friend, Sally's house. Sally had been a member of the development class. She was feeling low after her husband had left her, so Amy offered to sit with her. It was a small circle, just three permanent members, with the occasional visitor and they met weekly.

Before long, they began to experience flashes of light as they sat in the darkened room. They investigated every possible cause, but could not find anything which could have been responsible for the lights. Eventually they accepted them as signs from spirit people that they were there. Soon they noticed that their hands were glowing white in the dark and Amy's fingers often became elongated. They were also aware of soft rapping in the room.

Brenda, the other member of the circle, often appeared to be transfiguring, but Amy was never sure that she was not seeing the faces clairvoyantly, because she and Sally never saw the same thing at the same time. They experimented with table tilting and were moderately successful, although Amy was never happy doing this. It did not necessarily mean that the table was being moved by spirit friends, as it could have been due to their own energies.

Although Amy had gained some knowledge, it was mostly theoretical, as she had not had an opportunity to extend her experience through circle work. The circles she had led were for beginners and developing mediums and she had to be alert in order to monitor the students during their meditation. The only time she was ever invited to join a circle, it was held on the same night as the development class. Some may have chosen to join the circle to further their own development. Amy was sorely tempted, but felt that she had an obligation to the class. They needed her, and teaching newcomers was what she wanted to do.

When she saw one of Sybil's courses advertised in the College brochure which dealt with circle work, she persuaded Sally and Brenda that they should all go. They were joined by another friend of Sally's and Amy drove them to Stansted Hall, where they enjoyed a week of fun and discovery together.

Sybil was the course organiser and ran a tight, but happy ship. She was very experienced and seemed to be able to answer questions on any aspect of Spiritualist phenomena and philosophy. Amy knew that she wanted to be like Sybil, who was happy to share whatever she knew with others. There was no holding back and she was always ready to discuss anything, without patronising the student.

That course was the first of many that Amy attended. Sybil, recognising how serious Amy was about education, always had time to encourage and talk to her. For the first time since she walked through the door of a Spiritualist church, Amy felt that she was beginning to understand what Spiritualism was all about.

Meeting Sybil fuelled Amy's desire to teach. On Sybil's recommendation, she attended a course which dealt with the philosophy and science of Spiritualism. It was there she realised, for the first time, that she really was a medium and not just a psychic.

During this course, they took part in experiments in remote viewing and other psychic phenomena. Amy enjoyed the remote viewing, but found that she was much better at receiving the information than sending it. She was partnered with Bill, an elderly gentleman who had been a Spiritualist for many years. During this exercise one of each pair had to go out into the college, or its grounds, and concentrate on an object. The other had to remain in the college library and write down what he/she saw. Amy went out first.

She walked towards the sanctuary, where services were held, and looked out over the garden. She stood under a covered walkway and her eyes were drawn to the dovecote which was on a post in the middle of a small lawn, next to the sanctuary. She stared at it, taking in the shape and tried to blot everything else from her mind. She was on a time limit, and had to check her watch a number of times to make sure that she returned to the library within the specified time.

Bill read from his notes and roughly described the shape of the dovecote, but said he thought it was a clock. At first they thought that they had been unsuccessful, but when they talked later, they realised that Bill may have got the impression of a clock because of the times Amy had checked her watch. The shape of the dovecote also could have been mistaken for an old fashioned mantle clock.

Then it was Bill's turn to go out. Amy tried to clear her mind so that she could concentrate on the thoughts that Bill was sending back. It took her a while, but she felt the patina of oak, and could see an long, oval table. She wrote this in her notes and drew a picture of the table. She also included the fanciful thoughts she had had at the start, and waited for Bill to return.

He had only stepped into the gallery outside the library, and had concentrated on an oak gate-legged table which was very similar to Amy's sketch. He obviously was more disciplined than Amy, for he had not checked his watch at all and had concentrated on the table.

They returned to the library after lunch for another session in experimentation. The tutor, who was a past president of the Society for Psychical Research, had arranged twenty books in a bookcase. These were chosen at random and were numbered from left to right. They were hidden from the view of the students behind a blackboard. The students were asked to select a book by its number, choose a page and line, or paragraph number which would contain a message relevant to someone in the room. There were a total of twenty four people in the room, including Sybil and her assistant tutor, Eve.

The purpose of this exercise was to establish if there was an intelligence which was capable of knowing the contents of the chosen books and relaying this information to the students. This intelligent being might be referred to as a guide, or helper. This would also exclude the possibility of telepathy, for no-one, including the tutor, knew the content of the books.

Amy began to write immediately. In the space of ten minutes had three book references, along with notes concerning the content of the reference, and a drawing which had something to do with the recipient of the message.

As she was finished long before the others, Amy was allowed to read her first book reference. She had drawn a picture of a horse jumping a fence and said that she thought the message was for Eve. The book she had chosen was book number nine, page twenty six, first new paragraph. The book was 'The Manhood of Jesus' (vol. two.) As this was the second volume, the pages were numbered to follow those in volume one, so there was no page twenty six. Simon counted the pages, and on the twenty sixth page there was only one paragraph. It read:-

*'Now Shammai was a sage, and Jesus respected his wisdom, so he consented to go. Then, in his last night before his leave taking, his Father was with him and bade him return to Nazareth and there await a sign.'*

Eve said that this reading was very significant, as it confirmed a sitting she had received from Sybil that morning. Sybil had told her that she was searching elsewhere for wisdom, but had a lot of wisdom inside herself. Eve also confirmed that the drawing was significant, as she had done some show jumping when she was younger.

The next book that Amy chose was book number seven, page 134 beginning at the last paragraph. She had also drawn a baby in a crib to support the reading. Amy said that she thought the reading was for a woman who had lost a child when it was still in a crib.

One of the students, who had been a teacher, said that she had lost a baby, and had last seen the child alive in a crib. The seventh book was 'Love Conquers Death'. The last paragraph read:-

*'Between the ages of 3 and 17 the mind alters in a definite way. If a child comes here, say at three years old, the change called 'death' is a stop in the development of the mind. In your world at that age a child is growing rapidly and death stops temporarily its mental development because mental growth here is much more rapid than with you, so the child's mind must rest before it shoots ahead, and remains dormant for a period – the condition may last for at least a month, then it wakes up and becomes much more active than before death.'*

The woman stated that her baby daughter had passed away, aged six months, 37 years previously. The anniversary of this passing was the ninth of March, which was in three days time. The cot was significant to the woman, because she had knelt beside her baby daughter's cot and prayed on the night before the child died. She also felt that the text was particularly significant. As a teacher, the child's mind is important to her, and she had often thought about how her baby would progress mentally in the spirit world.

Not surprisingly, the woman was quite emotional, but pleased that she had received this answer to her questions. She had not mentioned this baby to anyone in the class, and even if she had, there was no way that anyone, including the person who had randomly chosen the books, could have known where the relevant text lay.

The last text that Amy had chosen was for herself. It was the fifth book, page seventeen, from row eleven. This was 'The Small Woman', by Alan Burgess. This book is the biography of Gladys Aylward, and the first full sentence on line eleven read 'Would you be prepared to consider the position?'

It was Amy's turn to become emotional, because she found the book itself particularly significant. Gladys Aylward wanted to be a missionary and to teach children in foreign lands. She was certain that she would do a good job because she cared deeply about these children. When she approached the Missionary Society they would not entertain her application because she was 'not qualified.' She persisted, returning to the Society each year, only to be turned away. Then one year they needed someone to assist a missionary in China and they sent Gladys.

Gladys was responsible for many reforms in China and she ran an inn where she found that she collected many orphans. When the Japanese invaded China she led these children to safety, travelling hundreds of miles across mountainous territory. Gladys did a wonderful job for one who was considered to be unqualified.

Amy felt that the text 'Would you be prepared to consider the position' might indicate that she may, one day, like Gladys, be rewarded for her persistence. She felt that this was a message from her spirit guide telling her not to give up and, like Gladys Aylward, if she continued to work hard she would eventually gain what she wanted.

This exercise was controlled by a scientist and the students did not know what form it would take. The books were chosen by the scientist at random, some from the college library, which has thousands of books. They were hidden from the students' view and they had no idea what experiment was to take place, so they could not prepare in any way. The fact that all of Amy's texts, and that the drawings she did related either to the text or to the recipients, is both unusual and remarkable. She had to obtain the information from somewhere, and it is feasible to assume that she was influenced in her choice of texts by an intelligence which would have known the content of the books. As Amy is a medium, this would point to her receiving the information from a discarnate spirit, possibly her spirit guide. She was happy to believe this, and it strengthened her belief that Mr. Latimer and Grey Wolf were indeed separate entities who guided and helped her through her earthly life.

She returned from the college that year with a new enthusiasm, but she soon came down to earth. Where could she practice these experiments? Who could she practice them with? Who was interested enough to help her to develop such a gift? The answer was that there was nobody who was dedicated enough or interested enough to help her. The opportunities were not there. Her life was full of other things and people who mattered to her, so she put her development onto the back burner.

The home circle should possibly have been somewhere to do this, but because there were only three of them, the scope would have been limited. Soon afterwards the circle broke up because, for various reasons, the three friends were not always able to meet. Something always happened to prevent one of them attending. Eventually they decided that this circle was not meant to be, and closed it.

# Chapter Eighteen

Amy was not to remain without a circle for long. Another medium, Alan, invited her to join his circle. She accepted on the condition that Pauline was allowed to sit too. After she sat with him for a couple of weeks it was obvious that the purpose of the circle was to develop Alan as a trance medium. She was happy to help him to do that and after a few weeks she asked if Sally and Brenda could join the circle to increase the energies needed to do this. Alan agreed.

This circle was short lived, too, lasting only a couple of months. However, it went on long enough to demonstrate that Amy was also a developing trance medium. Both Grey Wolf and Mr. Latimer spoke while she was in trance. She was disappointed that the circle had closed, as were her friends, but they could not find a place to hold a circle of their own, or even a time that suited them all.

Then, out of the blue, she received a telephone call from her cousin Steve. This was unusual, for she had not heard from him in years. They only usually spoke at family gatherings. Steve had begun to feel that he had something to do in his life other than the job he was doing as a gas fitter. He had attended a course in Shen healing and was determined to study this. He enrolled as a student and was seriously considering giving up his job when he qualified and was able to support himself as an alternative therapist.

Amy arranged to meet him at a local church. Pauline came, too, and at the end of the night they decided to meet at Steve's house and sit in circle there. They also invited Colin, a man whom Amy knew by sight, and Pauline had known previously. Amy suggested that Sally should be included in the invitation and they all agreed.

The circle met for two years. As Steve was a complete newcomer, it was initially a teaching circle with a guided meditation to music. Amy found that she had developed a new gentle way of teaching and was aware of a very patient spirit who helped her on these occasions. She could not put a face to him, but everyone was aware when he influenced her, because she was calm and knowledgeable. She was also aware of learning new teaching skills and wondered why she had not been aware of this spirit before.

It became obvious to Amy that Steve was a healer. She tried to encourage him to attend church and to develop this healing within Spiritualism, but he shied away from the religious aspect and the regulations which govern Spiritualist healers.

During the circle Amy found that she was impressed to draw faces while the others were meditating. Steve recognised one of them as the spirit he saw during his meditation and others were accepted too. There were also times when she went into trance, during which times it was usually Grey Wolf who spoke to the circle. Mr. Latimer only spoke on one occasion.

However, the circle appeared to be heading towards becoming a physical circle. There were lights which everyone saw, sometimes around the head of one of the sitters and there seemed to be ectoplasm forming within the circle. Amy introduced a bell and a trumpet into the circle and stood them on a piece of card which was marked around their bases to show their exact position at the beginning of the circle. None of them ever appeared to move, but at one point, after a year, a white steam, which was probably ectoplasm, collecting around the trumpet and went into or out of the mouthpiece. Everyone saw this, so it can be assumed that it was physical phenomena.

Amy went to the college for another of Sybil's courses. While she was there she received a spirit assessment from Dolly, Sybil's sister, and through this she discovered the identity of the spirit who helped her with her teaching. It was a monk, presumably the one she had seen at the séance when she had gone with Val to visit a medium for the first time. Things fell into place, for he must have been very patient, waiting all these years for Amy to recognise and acknowledge him. He transferred that patience to her while she was teaching.

After about a year she was also asked to take a development class in the church of which she was a member, so the opportunities to teach were beginning to present themselves. She was like a dog with two tails, and threw herself into her work.

Geoff was not pleased at this extra commitment, for it meant that Amy was spending four evenings a week either sitting in circle, teaching or taking services. She could not manage to open or close the garage door, as her shoulder was painful and stiff. This meant that she had to be home at a reasonable hour, so that Geoff did not have to wait up to put the car in the garage. Colin came up with the solution. He offered to give her a lift when they sat in circle and to bring her home afterwards.

************************

It had been seven years since Tim's death and Amy still thought about him. She often wondered why she was not aware of the dog who had been her devoted companion throughout his physical life. She had only seen him once, shortly after his death, and had become very emotional as a result. His daughter, Dolly 'popped in' now and then, but Tim was conspicuous by his absence. This made Amy wonder if all dogs and all humans really did survive their physical death. Of all her dogs, Tim was the one that she expected to be aware of. She was disappointed when he did not even come for a visit. Was he off chasing spirit rats? Was there somewhere where dogs like Tim go, perhaps to evolve?

Then one night, Amy had one of her 'vision' dreams. She dreamed that as she was walking up the stairs to bed she felt something brush against her leg. Afraid, she kicked out and looked back to see what it was that had touched her. Tim was falling down the stairs. Worried that she had hurt him, she ran to the foot of the stairs and picked him up. She cradled him in her arms and he looked up at her, love and devotion in his eyes as usual.

The content of her dream remained with Amy when she woke up. After thinking about it she realised that her doubts had been unfounded. He had never left her: she had just been unaware of his presence. The dream showed her that she had been pushing him away. How puzzled he must have been when she rejected him. Yet, with the same tenacity and unswerving devotion he had shown in his physical life, he stayed with her until she allowed him near once more.

Discarnate spirits, including dogs, communicate in various ways. They want to talk to us, to help and advise us. In order to receive this help and advice we need to listen. Communication is a two way thing. If we do not talk to spirits and give them the time and opportunity to reply, how can we expect them to answer?

You may think that, as a Spiritualist medium who regularly obtained evidence of soul survival for others, Amy should never have doubted that her dog was in the spirit world too. We must not forget that mediums are human, and emotions often play a big part in this. They are good at giving advice and comfort to others and not so good at practicing what they preach. A medium often needs a message relayed to them by others more than the general public does. To doubt is human, but whenever Amy doubted, her spirit friends always found a way of restoring and strengthening her belief. She realised that she had got into the habit of 'closing up' when she was not working in the Spiritualist churches which she served. Because of this she had locked Tim out, becoming unaware of her faithful little dog. Tim was a terrier by breed and tenacious by nature. He found a way of reaching his beloved mistress in the only way he could: through her dreams.

Spiritualists believe that the human soul survives physical death and continues to exist and progress in spirit form in a spirit world, retaining its individuality and personality into eternity. Perhaps that is also true of dogs, for Tim's persistence showed that his personality had not altered after his physical death. He retained all the characteristics that made him so endearing to Amy in life.

**********************

One by one their dogs aged, died and their remains joined Tim's in the garden. When Harry, the youngest and the last of the line, had to be put to sleep after a stroke, Geoff and Amy decided they would not have another dog. They had not realised the freedom they were granting themselves by not having an animal in the house.

They were able to go away together, and chose to visit Susan for a few days. She lived three hundred miles away, but they had a good car and they were both drivers, so they did not mind the journey.

Susan was head lass at a racing stable and lived on the premises with her dog, Jerry, a retired greyhound. Gerry was an accomplished thief, and was an expert at getting into cars and stealing whatever was edible.

Amy wandered around the stable yard and looked at some of the horses. She found that she was able to tune in to some of them, and was aware of their problems and temperament. One mare, who had won races the previous year but none in the current season, gave her the feeling of being disenchanted. As Amy stood in the box with the mare she felt as if she was part of the horse, and described characteristics which Susan said that the mare had recently developed. Amy felt that this mare was out of love with racing and would never win another race. She was broody, and wanted a foal. She told Susan this, and how the mare gave her the feeling that she needed to be retired to stud. Susan said that this would be unlikely to happen.

The few days they had with their daughter cheered Amy and Geoff up. She seemed to be settled in her job, and had lots of friends. She lived in a beautiful part of the country and although her lifestyle was simple, it was what she wanted. A few months later she had a serious riding accident.

The accident should have prevented her from working for many months, but that would have been in a 'normal' job. Working with horses is different, and although she was unable to ride, Susan hardly missed a day on the yard. Someone had to feed the horses and supervise any medication. In any racing stable, the head lad or lass is the cornerstone around which everything else is built. It was even more so in this case, for the yard Susan worked in was a small one, and there was no-one who could deputise for her.

Despite having a successful start to the season, the yard was in trouble. Susan's accident was the final straw. The trainer had nobody in the yard capable of doing her job, and decided that he would soon have to call it a day. Susan became redundant. Not only would she lose her job, but her home as well. Where could she go with a large dog like Jerry? She called her parents.

*"Come home,"* said Geoff

Susan did not want to do this. She explained that she had made her life in that part of the country and all her friends were there. However, she did not know where she was going to go, especially with Jerry.

"*We'll have him,"* suggested Amy, without hesitating. *"He knows us, and we've got plenty of room."*

They drove there and back in a day, with Amy doing most of the driving. Jerry was a good traveller, and they would not have known that he was stretched out in the back seat had it not been for his flatulence. The front windows of the car stayed down all the way home. Three hundred miles is a long way when you're trapped in a car with a flatulent dog.

Jerry settled in well and did not appear to miss the freedom he had experienced in his previous home. His presence gave Geoff a new lease of life, for he took the dog for a walk in the fields three times a day, whatever the weather. Jerry loved these walks, and the moment Geoff stood up and opened the cupboard under the stairs where the lead was kept, the dog bounced up and down with excitement, often launching himself at Geoff in his joy. Geoff thought this was wonderful, because Jerry was nearly twelve, a tremendous age for a greyhound.

The only thing Jerry enjoyed more than his walks was eating. The old dog was an incurable thief and had to be watched closely. He was able to open the fridge, so until they bought a child lock, the doors had to be taped shut. It was like having a new child. Both Amy and Geoff doted on the dog. Amy made him a tartan coat and Geoff never tired of telling anyone who would listen what a good dog he was. Because of Geoff's high opinion of Jerry, Amy laughingly christened him Jerry the wonder dog.

One morning, while Amy was getting dressed, Geoff called up the stairs to tell her that he was taking the dog for a walk. Jerry commenced to spring into the air and, as Geoff reached into the cupboard to get the lead, jumped up at him. Geoff held onto the lead, which was hanging on the back of the cupboard door, and the door swung closed, locking him inside. His knocking and shouting brought Amy downstairs, but, because of her arthritis, it took some time. Where, you may ask, was Jerry the wonder dog? Why had he not raced up the stairs to alert Amy, and bring help to his master? The simple answer was that he was in the kitchen, emptying the fridge.

# Chapter Nineteen

It seemed that Amy was finally getting her life together and everything was going her way. She was teaching, the home circle was going from strength to strength and, after ten years of working as a medium, she had finally taken the step of applying for a certificate of recognition from the SNU, She passed. This success spurred her on to do more and she picked up a correspondence course on world religions which she had put to one side, half finished, and began to work on her education.

Geoff was proud of her when she gained her certificate and encouraged her in her studies. Although he did not share her beliefs, he believed in her. They had been together for thirty two and a half years and he knew what she was capable of. Most of all, he knew that it made her happy, so that was fine by him.

She sometimes felt guilty that he spent so much time alone in the evenings while she was out at church. He did grumble now and then, but never stood in her way if she wanted to go somewhere. It might have helped if they could have had a holiday together, but either finances or babysitting commitments, or a combination of the two always prevented this.

By now Amy's arthritis had spread. Her hands were affected as well as her knees, ankles, shoulders and back. Geoff would not allow her to do any jobs around the house, and even started to make meals after her wrists gave way as she attempted to poach an egg, resulting in a second degree burn on her stomach. He became her carer and minder. I say minder because he always had to check that she had taken her medication at the right time.

He was a very meticulous man in every thing he did. Even when he put the car in the garage, he locked it firmly before locking the garage too. He left nothing to chance, and always double checked on whatever Amy did, for she often forgot things.

Now that he had retired they had more time together. They spent a lot of time in the garden, which they both loved. Amy did the planning and Geoff did the work and they enjoyed working together as a team. Their garden was secluded, with apple trees, a cherry tree, and a gooseberry bush. They also had a plum tree in a large pot. They filled the bird table every day and hung feeders with peanuts and fat balls in the trees. As a result they had a variety of birds who visited on a daily basis who they regarded as their pets.

There was only three years left to pay on their mortgage and they both looked forward to being better off financially when it was finished. Amy suggested that when this happened they would go away for weekends together, starting with a trip to the Norfolk broads. Geoff loved boats and fishing. She felt it was time that his interests and hobbies were put first. Besides, they could take Jerry with them onto a boat. Other than his obsession with food, he was well behaved and it would be something they would all enjoy.

Amy had an appointment to see her doctor on Christmas Eve that year to discuss the results of some tests. He told her she was diabetic. She was going to have to lose a lot of weight and change her diet. Ruefully, she looked at the sweets and chocolates she had already purchased for the festive season, wondering if she could resist the temptation to eat them. Friends and relatives had also bought gifts of chocolates for her, which she gave to Teresa. As always, Geoff was a tower of strength and was there for her whenever she was tempted to stray from her diet.

Shortly after Christmas, Amy woke in the middle of the night to find a large orange ball of energy next to her bed. She watched it for some time, mentally asking why it was there. All she got was that it was for strength. It was at least three feet in diameter and almost filled the space between the dressing table and her side of the bed, glowing and pulsating. She thought that perhaps it was there to help her to cope with her diabetes.

Sybil telephoned one day to ask Amy if she would like to do a workshop at a five day seminar she was running in July. Amy was delighted.

*"What subject?"* she asked

*"Anything you want,"* replied Sybil. *"How about doing an experimental workshop?"*

*"I'd rather do one on philosophy,"* Amy said. *"I feel that there aren't enough philosophy workshops these days."*

*"I'll put you down for that then,"* said Sybil. *"I'll send you the full programme nearer the time."*

Although she would only be working on one of the five days, Amy decided she would like to attend the whole seminar. It was just too far away for her to be comfortable in travelling every day, especially as there were services on each evening. She would have to stay there, which would mean that Geoff would be alone for a week. She had already booked a course at Stansted Hall in February, so how could she expect him to say that she could attend both. Why did she feel guilty when he said she should go?

Her trip to Stansted Hall, on the philosophy course, was educational and pleasant, but she was glad to get home. Geoff was not looking very well, and he was tired. Her tower of strength needed looking after. It was another week before he admitted that he was losing large quantities of blood from his bowels. Amy telephoned the doctor immediately and arranged an appointment for him.

The doctor said that he thought that Geoff might be suffering from interior piles, but would refer him to the local hospital for tests 'just in case'. Geoff could expect to hear from them within two weeks.

Amy was not convinced that the doctor's diagnosis was correct and knew in her heart that Geoff had cancer. Two weeks seemed like two years. They passed, and Geoff had not heard from the hospital. Amy urged him to ring the surgery. The receptionist stated that there was no referral on Geoff's notes, but she would rectify that immediately. She explained that they were in the process of moving and did not have a typist.

During the time they had to wait for the appointment, Geoff's condition deteriorated. He was passing blood and foul smelling black slime in alarmingly large quantities. By the time the letter came from the hospital he was very weak and they were both stressed. The letter did not make them feel any better. It stated that, because the clinic he had been referred to was very busy, rather than send him a remote appointment they would write to him six weeks before his appointment was due. They were both shocked. Amy picked up the phone and handed it to Geoff.

"*Make another appointment to see that doctor,*" she said. "*And tell him how bad it is.*"

Amy still had services to take. Mary, the wife of the president of the church she went to that weekend asked why she was looking so worried. Amy told her, swearing her to secrecy because she did not want Geoff's illness to become common knowledge. Sympathy always made Amy cry, and she could do without that. Mary urged Amy to make a private appointment to see a specialist. Amy, feeling guilty that she had spent their spare cash on her trip to Stansted, did not reply. Mary took her silence as a sign that she could not afford a private consultation.

"*I've got some money saved up,*" she said. "*You're welcome to that.*"

Amy felt humble at Mary's concern and generosity. This was what Spiritualism and the Brotherhood of Man was about.

"*Thanks, but I'll see if the letter comes in the next few days,*" she replied.

The letter arrived two days later, and Geoff was quickly diagnosed as having a malignant tumour in his colon. It was not far advanced and the surgeon said he would operate to remove it. The prognosis was good and they all felt better. Even so, Amy felt that she should cancel the workshop she had arranged with Sybil. She wanted to spend as much time with Geoff as was possible. She also cancelled the home circle and stopped going to church to help with the open circle.

Susan came to see her father as soon as she heard about his illness, then again on his birthday, which was in July. She brought Paul, her partner with her. It was the first time her parents had known about Paul, and they both agreed that he and Susan seemed well suited. Theirs had to be a fleeting visit, but it made her parents feel better that she had someone to share her life with.

Amy noticed that Geoff was quietly going around the house, doing jobs which would make her life easier. He mended the garage door and fixed it so that she was able to open it, despite her bad shoulders.

Geoff's operation was scheduled for the beginning of August. Ten days before he was due to be admitted, Jerry became ill. He was fine one moment, and enjoyed his morning walk then he started to vomit. He died overnight. The front garden was over populated with terriers, so Geoff lifted some flagstones in the back yard and buried the old dog there. Amy felt that her spirit friends knew she would be unable to exercise Jerry while Geoff was recovering after his operation and had called him home.

Geoff's elder sister, Rita, came to stay at the end of July. One of her sons brought her in his car, along with his sister, her son and his sister in law. With Teresa and Daniel, who was now nine, there would be eight for Sunday lunch. Teresa came to help and suggested that they take two joints out of the freezer. It was just as well they did, for on Sunday morning Amy's mother telephoned. Amy's niece, her husband and two small daughters were visiting from Germany, could they come for a visit? Amy was delighted, for she had not seen Julie for some time.

*"Of course they can,"* she said. *"We'd love to see them. Come for lunch."*

Now there were ten adults and four children. It was a good job they had a large extending dining table which accommodated the adults, while the children ate at a small table in the adjoining living room.

It was a wonderful day and everyone enjoyed themselves. Geoff and Stefan climbed ladders into the cherry tree to harvest the fruit, much to the delight of the children. Julie had a digital video camera and captured the day on film. When everyone had gone home the house seemed strangely quiet. Only Rita remained to stay with Amy while Geoff was in hospital. They visited him every day with Daniel and Teresa. Rita commented that Amy was being lax by leaving the car keys in the car and not shutting the side door of the garage, which was in the back yard. Amy replied that it was highly unlikely that anyone would climb over the high yard wall to steal their old car. She reasoned that if the keys were in the car, she would not have to waste time looking for them.

Geoff had his operation on the following Tuesday and it was pronounced to be a success. The prognosis was good, for the tumour was localised. Depending on the results of the biopsies, there seemed no reason why Geoff should not make a complete recovery.

The news cheered Amy, for she had been worried that something might have gone wrong. As the days passed Geoff grew stronger and by Sunday he was talking about coming home. That night he started having breathing difficulties and within twenty four hours he died.

# Chapter Twenty

Geoff's death was a shock to Amy and all her family. She had never visualised a life without him. Thirty three years is a long time to spend with anyone, especially someone like Geoff. They had been two halves of a pair, and for a while Amy wondered how she was ever going to cope without him. She felt guilty that she was not with him when he passed over, she knew that he would have been with her had their roles been reversed.

Pink roses were a special memory between Amy and Geoff, and his coffin had been draped with them. She also kept a vase of pink roses beside his photograph, next to 'his' chair, which she now sat on. The roses were not expensive and came from a local supermarket. They usually lasted about ten days, and she always replaced them before they wilted, so were good value.

In the days following the funeral Amy received fewer visitors and eventually she had to face being on her own. This was something she had dreaded, for she had never spent a night alone in the house. Strangely, she did not feel afraid or lonely.

One thing did bother her. Her relationship with Geoff had been so close that she had expected to feel the awful pain in her chest that she had felt after Tim had died. She expected to grieve, or at least be aware of grieving, but it did not happen. Of course, she was sad and missed Geoff greatly, but she had none of the pain which she'd experienced before.

She felt it was possibly because she had progressed since Tim's death. Her knowledge that the human soul survives physical death helped her. She knew that Geoff was continuing with his life and progressing in the spirit world. She would have to continue her physical life without his physical presence. How could she stand on the platform of a Spiritualist church and preach that life was eternal, that departed loved ones were only a thought away and not believe what she was saying herself? One thing was certain. He would not be far away. Looking after her was his prime concern and she could sometimes feel that he was near her.

She continued to leave the keys in the car while it was in the garage because she had a bad memory and did not want to spend time trying to remember where she had put them. After a while, even though she could swear that she had left them in the car, when she got in it they were not there. She searched the house from top to bottom but could not find them. Sighing, she took the spare set of keys from the cupboard and drove to her appointment. When she returned she tidied her bedroom and vacuumed the floor. While she was doing this she had to lift an extension lead to clean under it.

The missing keys still had not turned up by bedtime and it crossed Amy's mind that Geoff would have been concerned over their loss. She turned out the lights and went upstairs to bed. There, draped across the extension lead, were the missing keys. She went downstairs and checked to see that the spare set were where she had put them, which was in the cupboard, then went to bed, smiling.

*"You old villain,"* she laughed. *"All right, I'll not leave them in the car again."*

From then on she found herself talking to him, sharing moments when she watched the television programmes they had both enjoyed watching together.

She did not know how she would feel about going back to church. She had cancelled two services since Geoff had died and did not have one for another three weeks. The only problem was that her first one would be in the church where his funeral service had been held, so she was not sure if she could manage to do it. However, losing Geoff did not mean that she would give up her work. That would have been the last thing he would want her to do. She made up her mind to wait until nearer the time before she cancelled any more services.

She got into a routine where she took her medication with her breakfast and knew if she had forgotten them because they were in a box which was divided into the days of the week. However, when she contracted an infection in the nail bed of her big toe, she had to have antibiotics which she needed to take four times a day. These were trickier, for they had to be taken on an empty stomach and she did not always remember to take them. One evening she went to bed with the bottle and a glass of water because she had missed a dose. Her idea was to read for an hour or so then take the tablet.

Reading in bed always made Amy sleepy and it was not long before she was sound asleep. She woke up with a start in the middle of the night, aware that there was a strange noise. The house next door was divided into two flats and the man in the upstairs flat played in a band, so often came home early in the morning. His living room was on the other side of Amy's bedroom wall, so she often heard him quietly talking. She strained her ears to listen, thinking that, if he had not made a noise, then she might possibly have an intruder.

Then she heard the pills being rattled in their bottle. She looked at the clock. It was exactly four hours since she had taken the last one. She felt comforted, feeling that the pills had not rattled themselves, so Geoff must have been there to make sure she took her full dose.

Geoff's death had brought another of Amy's daughters back into her life. Maria came to the funeral and visited a few times afterwards, to support her mother. Although she had not lived with her mother and Geoff, she had on occasions visited them. She approved of him, for it was plain that he and her mother were happy, but what she really liked about him was his sense of humour and the way he teased her whenever she telephoned to speak to Amy.

Amy knew she would eventually go back to church, but was unsure how she would cope. Sympathy always made her feel sorry for herself and she knew that her friends in the church would want to express their support by hugging her. Hugs are mandatory in a Spiritualist church, and although Amy had got used to this practice, she felt that these expressions of friendship and brotherhood might start her tears flowing. At the same time, she missed going to the church and she knew that Geoff would want her to continue to live her life as normally as possible.

She decided that an open circle would be the best time to go back. It was a more informal gathering than a Sunday service and she could always leave the circle if she felt weepy. Once she had made her decision she acted on it immediately and went to church.

There were expressions of sympathy, but it was reasonably low key because she had warned the church president in advance that she needed a little space. Amy had not planned to work that night, but there were not many mediums at the circle. Nevertheless, she was more surprised than anyone when she got to her feet during the service and gave a message. She received a message from another medium and at the end of the night was glad she had made the effort to attend.

She lingered in the church after the service, enjoying the company of other members and visitors over a cup of tea. She had left a standard lamp on in the living room to deter possible burglars, so did not bother to put the main light on, she sat in Geoff's chair for a few moments, going over the events of the evening. She looked at the clock. It was late and she felt tired. There would be no need to read in bed tonight. As she turned the lamp off, her attention was drawn to the roses. They looked different, but she put that down to the fact that the lamp did not illuminate every corner of the room.

The next day she could not believe her eyes. It had not been a trick of the light. Geoff's roses had turned from pink to violet. They were only a couple of days old, so they were still very fresh and they had come from the same supermarket as the others.

She telephoned everyone she thought might be interested and showed the flowers to Teresa. Between them they tried to come